Laura Ellen Joyce researches 21st century literature, necrophilia, masculinity, crime scenes and pornography at Sussex University. She is project co-ordinator of the AHRC Global Queer Cinema project. She has been published in *Succour*, *Paraxis* and *Quick Fictions*, and anthologised in *Murmurations: An Uncanny Anthology of Bird Stories*. She lives in Brighton.

laura ellen joyce
the museum
of atheism

SALT

CROMER

PUBLISHED BY SALT PUBLISHING
12 Norwich Road, Cromer, Norfolk NR27 0AX

© Laura Ellen Joyce, 2012

Salt Publishing 2012

Printed in Great Britain by Clays Ltd, St Ives plc

Typeset in Paperback 9/10

ISBN 978 1 907773 14 3 paperback

1 3 5 7 9 8 6 4 2

For my grandparents Ellen, Joe, Margaret and Trevor

CONTENTS

MUSHROOM SOIL

The sunken garden was in full bloom. Soft mossy banks dipped low to the soil and dark green liquid crept down through the humus. A sharp smell drifted up through the glass roof, to the prison above. To the dark concrete basement that shut out all daylight when there was any. In December, Rosewood had no sun at all.

The soil was richer than anywhere else in the state. The bones of hundreds of foxes were ground up and fed to the sunken garden, their blood captured in vials and stirred through the earth. There was a creeping liquefaction under the garden that bubbled and pulsed, dripping slow as a coffee pot through the putrid soil. The earth was writhing with life, with maggots and larvae and blowflies, with ticks and beetles and lice.

Once there was the body of a girl in the sunken garden. A dead blonde girl. She lay on her side, one arm missing. Bluish tangles of veins were exposed at the knotted edge of the butchered place. Blood seeped through, a milky red that furred the wound shut. Beneath her neck, a mess of blood pooled through the mossy ground. Maggots curled lazily though her pink flesh below, roiling, rolling, bloated with meat they slowed and stopped just short of the opened brain. Violet scum bubbled out and formed a hard shimmering caul like blown glass. The mess of maggots gave off a white heat that scorched her flesh. Her intestines were spilling out and plastic bullets shirred the rubbery meat. A man came, and turned her face to the dirt. He covered over all that rot.

The harvest that year was spectacular. Ghost Fungus and Witches' Butter, Vinegar Cups and False Deathcaps thrived where they should not have done: In basements, in attics, creeping up walls. They flourished that winter under neon skies, lit red by the northern lights, as the sunken garden pulsed underground.

PART ONE: PLAYING DOCTOR

0800 24 DECEMBER – 1900 24 DECEMBER

24 DECEMBER 0800

Rose Cap
Appearance: Milky pink caps, thin stem.
Effects: Induces hallucinations.
Environment: Near water.

Jed Wilde was bone tired. He'd been out in the valley hunting foxes all night, and his shirt was spattered with their blood. He was drenched in sweat from the struggle and he knew it would turn to ice on his skin if he didn't get back in the truck and drive home soon. The needle on the thermometer in the cab was busted, but he didn't think it was going to creep much above freezing that day.

Leo, Leo, come on we've got to get home. Jed called to his boarder, who was sitting hunched on his hind legs, smoking a cigarette. Leo didn't reply at all.

What's wrong with you? Jed asked, D'you want to stay here like this all day? We should get back to the house. Come on.

Leo threw the cigarette end into the new drift of snow that covered the forest floor. It hissed and went out. He stood up, legs shaking, and followed Jed to the truck. They had trouble starting the engine and Leo grabbed their coats and some blankets from the back under the tarp while Jed gave it some juice.

The truck started after a couple of good hard revs. They began the journey back to the house. Leo reached out for the radio dial until he found a sports bulletin amongst all the Christmas carols and adverts.

Would you turn that off? Jed asked him. I need to concentrate on driving. I'm not getting much traction in this snow.

Alright pussy. Want me to drive?

Yeah, I don't think that's a good idea.

Leo didn't argue. He shivered, as though catching a chill. He turned off the radio and wrapped the blankets more tightly around his body; then started snoring loudly. Jed turned the radio off. It was difficult to get the truck up the steep curve of the valley. Slicks of black ice layered the highway, fresh snow covering the grit laid earlier. Jed had to concentrate on the ascent and he was thankful that Leo's presence was muted by sleep. The valley had been drained, years ago, and there was no water at the bottom any longer, just flat lands with a few small houses. The main heart of Rosewood was on the north side of the valley; that was where the Fantasy Bar was, and the strip of stores and most of the housing clustered round the town hall. But Jed liked the south side. He could see all the way over, see everything that was happening, and if he saw a car making its way across he could be gone before they arrived. Usually, the trip from the base of the valley to his house took less than ten minutes in the car, but this fucking ice was a nightmare, the street lighting at the bottom of the valley was out, and he was sick of seeing nothing in front of him but his headlights day and night.

A scream rang out across the valley and Jed jumped in his seat, letting the stick shift slip out of his control.

Fuck was that? Leo muttered, not opening his eyes.

Fox, Jed said, concentrating on getting the car under control.

Jed went in to his daughter's bedroom as soon as he got home. He wondered what Ava might have heard in the night.

Ava, darling? Jed called to her softly to check if she was awake. He couldn't stop shaking and thought she would notice something was wrong. He realised that he might frighten her, dressed as he was, so he went down to the basement to take off his bloody clothes and change them for fresh ones. Leo had already dumped his clothes and the dirty blankets in the washing basket. Jed took off his boots and laid them on a sheet of newspaper. Then he went up to the kitchen and made Ava's oatmeal.

Upstairs, in his daughter's room, Jed got in beside her and tickled her on the chin to wake her up.

Daddy! She said in surprise. He offered her the oatmeal and she said she didn't like the taste this morning. Jed played a game with her where he breathed hot steam from his coffee right into her mouth and she gulped it down like a magic potion. Jed looked at the sky outside lit by the northern lights; it was a weird colour, like raw pigs' liver.

Ava was in her pajamas and still half-asleep. Jed smoothed her hair where it curled and brushed it away from her face. He had a lot to do but he couldn't resist her asking for just one story. As he unplugged her star nightlight, the fading gleam lit his hand red for just a second. She waited for the story to begin.

Tell me one about the foxes Daddy, Ava said. She was scared of the foxes but she liked to hear about how her daddy fought them and kept her safe.

Jed wondered how much she knew. He told her the safe story, the one he had told her before.

One day an airplane came over the valley. The pilot had never flown a plane before and he had a dangerous cargo. Remember what a cargo is sweetie?

Ava told him she remembered. It was the stuff he was carrying. She wasn't a baby, she told him, she knew this story already. Jed laughed at her seriousness.

Well this cargo was kind of dangerous. It was absolutely full to the brim of chemicals. Chemicals which did strange things to the foxes.

Ava pretended to shiver in fear and crept closer to her

Daddy. He dropped his voice low.

The plane began to get into trouble and the pilot wanted to save himself so he let the cargo fall out of the bottom of his plane. A terrible green slime came out of the sky like rain and began to drip down into the valley. All of the trees in the forest were covered and the birds perching in the branches were stuck fast. The other animals took shelter until the terrible storm was over, all except the foxes. Do you know why?

Ava knew why, she said, because they wanted to eat the birds and they were too greedy.

That's right. They wanted to eat the birds and they were too greedy so they shook the trees until the slime-covered birds fell down in front of them. They ate every last bird.

And then they grew big, like monster foxes and started stealing the baby lambs! Ava said, remembering her favourite part.

And that's why you had to wear your wellingtons every day, even in the hot summer. Because if you put your foot in that slime then you might turn into a monster too! Jed growled and tickled Ava, pretending to eat her up. She squealed and laughed. But he knew there was something about the story she didn't like, she was not much bigger than a lamb herself. If it meant she stayed away from the toxic waste, then so much the better.

Tell me another one Daddy; tell me the story about the goddess who brings the sunrise.

Jed picked Ava up and took her over to the window so they could see the sky.

Aurora, the goddess of the dawn, ran away from her husband every day. She made a damned fool out of him.

Ava giggled when he swore. He didn't normally do it in front of her but she had heard him swearing with his friends. With Leo.

Her husband was jealous because he was old and she was young and wanted all the young men. All the beautiful gods.

Ava didn't understand what jealousy was or even who all

the gods were but she saw how powerful his words seemed. Jed paused.

But this goddess Aurora, it didn't matter that she made a fool out of her husband. It didn't matter because of how beautiful she was. When she travelled across the sky her fingers trailed pink stardust through the early morning clouds and brought hope to the world.

He could hear his voice sounded funny. He knelt beside Ava and pointed outside.

But she doesn't come in wintertime?

No Ava, sweetie, she sleeps tight in wintertime. But look at what she sends instead. Those are Aurora's fingers now.

Jed and his daughter looked out of the window together, seeing the pale pink glow in the corner of the sky, like a peeled lychee. The northern lights were brighter this year, bright enough to dwarf the miserable amber fuzz from the streetlights. Jed was scanning the ground for foxes and Ava was looking at the snowy sky, trying to catch a glimpse of the goddess.

Finish your breakfast darling and I'll be back soon I promise. Daddy's got some work to do. Jed said.

He messed up her hair and she pushed his hand away. He didn't seem to mind and she watched him turn the handle and walk out of the door, leaving a dark stain on the brass handle.

Caroline's still in bed. She said she's not feeling too good. Jed told Leo.

Well I'm not too hungry now anyway. Could do with some coffee though. You?

Jed nodded, took the newspaper from his friend and began reading it. He put his stockinged feet up to the stove which he'd lit earlier for the oatmeal. They were still cold in spite of being in bed with Ava.

Leo let coffee drip into the pot on the stove and took two pint mugs down from the dresser. He took whiskey from his flask and poured an inch into the bottom of his.

You? He asked Jed.

Jed didn't look up from his reading but shook his head.

Leo poured the rest into his own mug and replaced the flask in his trouser pocket.

So Jed, what were you doing up there with Caroline? Do I need to ask?

I went in to see Ava.

Ava? Leo asked.

Yeah, you know how she is; she looks out of that window sometimes and sees what she oughtn't. I wanted to check she had been asleep.

And was she?

I think so.

What about the little faggot?

What did you call Jonny?

Oh so you knew who I meant. Leo laughed at this. He laughed and poured coffee.

Jed did not thank him when the mug was placed next to him on the table.

Can I get the financial section? Leo asked.

Jed pulled it out of the centre of the newspaper and handed it over, still not looking up.

Thanks. Leo smiled, pulling the blanket he was still wearing tight around his shoulders. He gulped the coffee back in one and bent down next to the stove, spreading the newspaper on the floor so he could polish his boots.

You're not going to the prison today? Jed asked. Looking like that?

It's not a full shift, just a little something for the governor.

You can't seriously go to work in this state Leo.

Couple of hours tops. Don't worry. It's later tonight. I'll be at the pageant if that's what you're worried about. See Ava doing her stuff.

You know what I'm worried about. I'll take another cup of coffee if it's going.

Leo stood up from his job, took Jed's empty cup and filled it up. When he passed it back to him there were two perfect fingerprints in black polish on the white enamel surface. Leo went back to his boots and Jed finished reading the paper in silence.

24 DECEMBER 0900

False Deathcap
Appearance: Translucent grey base with deep white cup.
Effects: Eyes fill with blood, blistering of skin.
Environment: Dry walls.

One of Ava's legs was sticking out of her white cotton dress.
The leg was bare and bluish. Her dress was crisply ironed,
but it was far too cold for winter in the mountains. All around
her body a fuzzy outline of moisture surrounded her, like
crime scene chalk, where the heat of her body touched the
steel table top.

Now I take the scalpel and cut out part of your brain to
put in my jar.

Jonny, Ava's ten-year-old brother, was pretending to be a
doctor. He had his superman cape wrapped around him like
a gown and was wearing a pair of their father's old glasses
with thick brown rims.

What will you do with it Jonny?

Dr Jonny.

What will you do with it Dr Jonny? Ava giggled and twirled
her fake-platinum hair around her fingers.

I'm going to examine it to see if you have been taken over
by brain monsters! Aaaggghhhh!!!

Jonny leaned over and lifted up his little sister's dress and
blew raspberries on her stomach until she was laughing so

hard she could barely breathe.

Ava jumped down off the table and squirmed away from Jonny.

The dressing-up part of the room was her favourite bit. She knew she could hide there and Jonny wouldn't be able to find her. She squeezed under the piles of pageant clothes and stayed still, holding her breath. She loved the way her Christmas dresses sparkled like snow. She was annoyed that they were so scratchy though. She hated wearing the really big ones because they crackled under her arms and left little pink patches she wasn't allowed to scratch.

Ava thought Jonny didn't know where she went when she hid under the dresses. Jonny laughed to himself at how silly his little sister was. Six year-olds were such babies. He wanted to do another experiment on her and he had a way to make her come out. He didn't want her to know he could see her leg sticking out of the pile of dresses. Mom would be mad if she saw them playing in the basement with all of the important things in there ready for the parade that afternoon.

Ava? I can't see you. Where did you go? Jonny crept behind one of the dressmakers' dummies and made himself flat to the outline of the torso.

Ava! I think I've gone invisible. I ate one of the magic mushrooms and now I can't see my hands!

Jonny sounded scared. Ava was worried that she might be invisible too. What if they both disappeared?

Jonny? Ava ran out of her hiding place and with relief realised that she could see herself in the long mirror. Her ringlets were all tangled and she knew she'd get in trouble but she didn't care. Where was Jonny?

Ava, I think I've gone inside this dummy and I can't get out. Jonny pushed the dummy forward very slowly do that it looked as though it was walking towards her. It was one of the scariest dummies with its head hanging half off and one of the breasts detached. Their mom was going to mend it but she hadn't had time. There were so many things to do for

Ava's pageants that she was busy all day long. Jonny thought it would be stupid to believe that he had gone inside the dummy and he couldn't believe it was working.

Jonny? Are you okay in there? Do you want me to get Mom?

No. Don't leave me. I ate one of the mushrooms on the wall and now I've gone invisible. If you eat one too you can come and rescue me.

Jonny saw how brave and serious Ava looked and laughed out loud. The dummy wobbled and fell towards Ava. She sat flat on her butt and opened her mouth in shock, unable to make a sound. Jonny hugged her to him quickly before she could cry.

It's okay. You rescued me from the dummy. I'm safe now.

Jonny was safe and he pushed the icky dummy away. He picked Ava up and sat her back on the metal table. He put his glasses back on.

I need a patient to volunteer for a special experiment.

What's an experiment Dr Jonny?

It's a special test that doctors do. You can have a treat afterwards.

Ava opened her eyes wide, and forgot about her sore bottom.

Jonny was drawn to the sweet wetness of the fungus which grew in the corner of the basement. He took off one of his stick pins that held his cape together and speared it between his left finger and forefinger. He looked very carefully at the patterns on the wall. Their dad had told them never to touch it, but Jonny knew there were special mushrooms in amongst the dangerous ones. He had heard his dad and the others down here some nights and heard what they had said about the dreams the mushrooms gave them. If he pretended Ava had done it herself then no one would believe it was his fault.

From a distance the fungus looked like a ship's rigging, the black webs draped in folds along the walls. But up close, each one had a different shape. Some had long thin tails that looked like suckers with blotches of blood. Others looked like black roses, velvety to the touch. At the heart of these sat worms and grubs so that the petals soon became ragged and holey. The mushrooms Jonny was searching for were tiny crimson blobs no bigger than pomegranate seeds. Wherever the black ones grew so did they. Jonny found some and dropped them into his cupped palm.

Try one Ava; it looks like a little Christmas berry. I bet it's sweet.

Daddy said we weren't supposed to eat them.

He just said that to you because he thought you were a baby. You're not a baby are you?

Ava didn't always like it when Jonny was a doctor. Sometimes he was too stern about it. She didn't want to eat any icky mushrooms. She let out a scream before Jonny could put his hand over her mouth. But as she did, he dropped the handful of spores in her mouth. She spat them straight up to the ceiling where they stuck. One landed on the high window at the top of the basement, sliding down and leaving a bloody smear on the glass which was beginning to frost over with early snow.

The snow had been falling since dawn, and when Daniel Cooper got up at nine thirty, he could breathe the cold in. He had his thermals on, of course, but this mountain air chilled him. He wasn't a heavy man, no meat on him, and he had barely any appetite. He couldn't bear to get in the shower, so he just pulled on a second set of thermals and his dressing gown. He was careful to bend slowly when he put on his socks, every time he made a sharp movement he expected to seize up and stay bent double. He had slipped his disc three times, though he wasn't yet forty, and still couldn't force himself to keep up with the exercises from the doctor.

As soon as he had tea on the stove he felt better. The kitchen heated nicely and he sat letting the warm jasmine steam float over his face. He opened the drapes and watched as the snow settled. He lived on the north side of the valley, right at the edge of the drop. The kids were always hanging round his front garden because it had the best sledding in the whole of Rosewood. There were already a couple of kids in matching blue snowsuits trying it out. It wasn't his fault that their tree house had to be taken down when he moved in, it was Rosewood property now, and he'd been assigned the cottage. Before he moved in the place had been derelict and the kids used it as a hangout. That was why they were angry with him for moving in.

On top of all that, Daniel's was worried about his girls. If he kept them in the outhouse they might get damaged. It had been a hell of a job to get some of them in the kind of condition he'd managed and he didn't want to ruin a week's work now. His own girls, Lucy and Magdalena, always sat in the living room, but he wasn't sure how he felt about bringing the others in. It might not be quite right, especially at Christmas.

He put his wellingtons on and walked the ten yards to his workroom. The side of the building had been spray-painted with the same angry red words he'd cleaned with a rag and kerosene the week before. It might be time to think about moving on. He liked it here though, the clean air and the space to think. Better than the hot, dirty cities he'd been living in. Perhaps it was just kids. Kids pick on anyone. Besides, he always kept the workroom locked and no one would know about the girls. It was for their sake as much as his. He had to protect their dignity. Inside, his workroom was just as he had left it. Three realflesh dolls lay on their separate benches, each one as perfect as they had been when they were originally created. Daniel was an expert at seeing to all their little cosmetic procedures, from make-up and hair to more intimate areas. He didn't mind repairing and tightening the girls, but he felt disappointed when he considered how roughly they had been used. The words they'd sprayed last week applied more to the men who sent him these dolls to repair.

It's okay, I know you're cold out here so I'll bring you

inside. It's not nice to be out in the cold at Christmas.

Daniel took a long brown wig from a stand and arranged it carefully with pins on the first doll's head. He brought red and blonde wigs and dressed the other two as well.

I couldn't expect you to go in looking bald. I know these aren't yours but they'll do for now. I'll let the others know to expect you and then we can go in.

24 DECEMBER 1000

Milk Cap
Appearance: Tall blue-grey stalk. White fronds
Effects: Sweet flavor, edible.
Environment: Water and damp.

Ava sat quietly sucking her thumb as Jonny wrapped her up in the superman cape. He spoke roughly to her.

Ava, you have to stop being such a baby . . . How can I do experiments on you if you're going to make such a fuss? Now listen, why don't you be the doctor for a while? You can wear the glasses and examine me.

Okay. You have to call me Dr Ava though.

Sure Dr Ava. No problem.

What kind of examination are you going to do?

What do I have to do? Do I have to put the mushrooms in your mouth? I don't wanna. What is an examination anyway?

It's just looking at something carefully. Forget about the mushrooms. Stop talking about them.

Why? Why should I stop talking about them? You made me eat them.

I'll lie down and take my shirt off; you get one of the sheets from the dummies and put it over me. You can pretend I'm dead and you're doing an autopsy.

No I want to be dead! Let me be dead! I'm really good at lying still under the sheet. I can hide better than you!

Okay. But you have to do it right. Take off your dress so I can check your heartbeat and breathing. You need to be cold if you're really dead.

I don't mind. Ava said as she took off her dress and swapped places with Jonny on the table. She lay completely still and shut her eyes. She felt beautiful, like a picture of Jesus in the tomb she'd seen at church.

Jonny reached up to take the glasses from her.

Give me the glasses back so I can look at you properly.

No I don't want to, they're mine!

You can't be the doctor and the patient Ava. It's not fair.

Why not?

You're not dead now are you? I can hear you talking.

Jonny snatched the glasses and Ava began to cry and pulled the sheet over her head.

What are you two doing down there? You know how busy today is for me. Why can't you play nice together? Caroline shouted down the basement stairs. She arrived a minute later with a petticoat of gold gauze in her arms. Jonny stepped away from his little sister, grabbing a tissue from his pocket to clear away the dribble of mushroom mucus that had slid down the wall from the window.

Ava, what are you doing under that sheet? I need to fit you for your costume so get down to your underwear and come over to the mirror. Caroline chucked Jonny under the chin and gave him a little nibble on the ear. It's girl time now so why don't you go up and get some breakfast with Leo?

Okay Mom, said Jonny.

Ava unwound herself from the sheet and followed her mother over to the mirror.

Daniel thought how lovely the girls looked all sat together in the living room. He was so proud. He knew he was silly but they had been so good, good as gold with no tantrums or tears. He knew he was dealing with ladies.

I'm not going out for long this afternoon, I just think it

would be a crying shame to miss the Christmas pageant. All those baby beauty queens wrapped up like candy. I need some new ideas to keep you all looking fresh.

Daniel hesitated before explaining his plan to them, he had become nervous since the spray-paint incident, and the last thing he wanted was to make the girls nervous as well. They were so vulnerable. He really couldn't bear to miss the show though. He was going to keep the drapes closed for a while, maybe until the snow passed. They would be safer that way.

I thought it might be cosy to wrap up warm and close the drapes for the rest of the day – it's so dark anyway and I don't want you to catch a chill. I'll bring you in some blankets as well.

Daniel went to fetch the extra blankets from the attic. He was disturbed by the doorbell. He ignored it, glad he'd shut the drapes. He could hear laughter. Suddenly fearful, he slunk back down the stairs, and crawled down the hallway, so that whoever it was couldn't see him through the glass in the door. Before he reached the door he saw a lit sparkler drop through the letterbox. He grabbed the *Yellow Pages* from the hallstand and dropped it down hard enough to put out the flame. Daniel rose slowly and with effort, he realised how stupid he had been to crouch down in the first place. He had to be more careful. Thank God he was able to get up and walk okay.

Don't worry, nothing to be upset about, it's fine, just some silly children. Daniel went to calm Lucy and Magdalena. He did love the others but they weren't his own. Of course he didn't want anything bad to happen to the other three but he started wondering if they were bringing him too much attention. Perhaps he should have been more discreet with the workshop. Daniel was worried that there might be more to come. He walked to the kitchen stiffly and filled a pail with cold water to splash the carpet. He made sure the fire was really out before bringing the girls in some blankets and changing out of his soiled clothes.

Leo looked at the kid as he came in to the kitchen. He was such a pussy, not interested in going fishing or shooting. He was going to be hunting with them later that night, whether he wanted to, or not.

Morning Sport. How are you today? Finished playing dress up with your little sister? Jonny said nothing to this, didn't even go red like a normal kid would, He went over to the cupboard and poured a bowl of Ricicles as though Leo hadn't spoken.

Jonny thought about how stupid Leo was and how big and red and full of shit he seemed to be. He was always in the kitchen as well, sitting drinking coffee by the stove or polishing his prison boots on a bit of newspaper. Today he was taking a shotgun apart to clean and listening to a talk show on the radio. There was never any peace when he was around.

Hey. Hey hey hey I'm talking to you. You're coming out later with your dad and me. We're going to get those foxes tonight and you can learn how to handle a gun. I hope you're better at that than you are with a fishing rod.

It's too cold. It's snowing. I'm not going out with you.

Jonny got down from his stool at the kitchen table and picked up the cereal bowl to take it up to his room.

Going crying to Mommy? While you're there you can tell her that I pay enough fucking rent to expect clean sheets. Clean sheets every day. Why don't you go and help her with the laundry downstairs. You must be good for something.

Jonny realised that Leo must have been up all night. There was dribble on his chin and he smelled of whiskey. He walked quite quickly to his room and shut the door.

Daniel left the fire on one bar and the lamp on a warm glow. He felt bad leaving the girls but he didn't have many chances to see baby beauty queens. He couldn't really go to the main pageants because he wasn't with a family. At least on Christmas Eve most of the town was out, and visitors, so he could blend in. It wasn't because of the Rosewood pageant that he'd asked to be assigned accommodation in the valley; it was because of the chance to get out of the city. The scene that had grown up around Ava was phenomenal; she was such a little star that she drew the crowds alright. And the people in the town didn't seem to understand that using her beauty to make money themselves was no less filthy than the money changers in the temple had been. He didn't want any part in that, he just wanted a chance to look at her and the other beautiful little girls, to show his heartfelt appreciation. People didn't always understand.

Daniel wrapped up warmly and went outside to check if there were any more yucky surprises. When he was outside he saw what had drawn the attention of the boys and felt sick. No wonder that it made no difference how many times he locked the doors of the workroom and closed the drapes. With the pale drapes shut and the lamp on, the silhouette of five statuesque girls could be seen clearly. It was worse than before. Daniel went back into the house and locked and chained the door. He carried the girls one by one upstairs to his bedroom and piled them on to the bed.

I'm so sorry. I know this is undignified but we're not safe ladies. I'm going to have to go out and get some thicker drapes. He gave each of them a quick kiss and made his way quickly to the car.

Hold still Ava, how can I fit this dress properly if you keep moving?

Do I have to go to the parade? I'm tired.

You wouldn't be so tired if you didn't spend all morning fighting with your brother.

We weren't fighting, we were playing doctor.

Well whatever you were doing you've ruined a perfectly good dress and tired yourself out. And what is that on the ceiling?

Ava didn't know whether to tell her mother what had happened with the mushrooms. She thought Jonny might be mad at her so she kept quiet and still.

That's much better sweetie. Now I can do the other side.

Caroline tied gold ribbons around her daughters' waist until she looked like a little Christmas present to put under the tree. She would have loved to see her at the pageant, but it wasn't worth the trouble with Jed. They were both still and silent, looking at each other in the mirror until they heard Leo stumbling down the basement stairs demanding his breakfast.

24 DECEMBER 1100

Witches' Butter
Appearance: Shallow mustard-coloured bowls leaking green mucus
Effects: Vinegary Flavour, Stomach cramps and diarrhea.
Environment: The foot of weeping willows.

Caroline's a bit mean with the bacon isn't she? And how old is this coffee? Leo said to Jed as they sat in their undershirts at the kitchen table, bellies slopping over their shorts.

It wasn't the cooking you asked me about Leo. Are you seriously telling me that Maria would let you sit here at eleven o'clock in the morning drinking coffee in your underwear? If you ever want to go back to your wife just let me know.

Jed knew he wouldn't have anything to say to that. Leo's face flushed redder than usual, the broken veins that aged him seeming to spread.

I wouldn't go back to that dried up bitch, anything's better than that. You'd swear I was trying to kill her just getting a bit of loving.

Well you can't go wrong with Caroline there. So I wouldn't worry about her being mean with the bacon.

There was a long silence. It was shaky ground. Leo slapped the table a couple of times, and shivered, recovering himself.

Anyway, what about later, do you still fancy some sport? We need to get that kid of yours ready to handle a gun. He

24

spends too much time playing dollies with his sister. He cheeked me this morning. You've got to get him out in the fresh air or you'll have a little serial killer on your hands. That's how it starts, believe me.

Leo, you are full of shit. The kid's only ten years old. He'll be going to high school next year. Plenty of time to toughen up then. I don't want to bring him out with us tonight. We don't know how bad it might get.

Your call. But if you listen to me . . .

Yes it is my call. I'm going to get dressed. Maybe you should take a shower. You smell like a farm.

Jed stood up from the table and turned off the stove.

Ava darling you look beautiful. Let me just take this dress over to the sewing machine to run up the hem. You put your robe on and chose what make-up you want me to do.

Ava twisted the material between her fingers; she didn't know how to say what she wanted to.

Mommy do I have to go today? Can I go and play in the snow instead?

Ava sweetie, do you know how hard it was for me to get you into this parade? Only the best beauty queens can enter.

Ava knew that was a lie. She was always in the pageant. She never had any snow days.

But I want to make a snowman.

You can do that when you come home darling. Daddy and Leo will help you.

I don't want to do it in the dark. I don't like Leo's smell. He smells funny when he picks me up and his face is sharp, it itches me.

Ava. I'm not arguing with you about this. Please just decide on your make-up and I'll finish your dress. You know that if you go there'll be a present from Santa don't you?

Ava thought about this, she really did want a special present like she'd been promised; she just didn't want to have to stand up in front of everyone and twirl around. She was sick of getting her make-up done for hours and hours and sitting in the basement with her mother while she made dresses. She wanted to go sledding outside.

Is the present a sled?

What? Caroline asked through a mouthful of pins.

Will it be a sled so I can go sledding after, when the parade is over? Ava asked.

Yes. Caroline answered, and then the noise of the sewing machine cut through the basement, finishing the conversation.

That Leo is such a bastard, thought Jonny, as he sat reading his comics. I wish that Dismembered Man would come and destroy him, he thought. Dismembered Man was an unusual creature. He was an evil demon doctor who went around murdering and mutilating people to get body parts. He attached the pieces together to make a body for himself. The funny thing about Dismembered Man was that he liked to have new body parts all the time, that way no one ever knew what he looked like and he could give everyone an icky surprise. What part of Leo would he take? He wouldn't want his fat stomach or his ugly red face. Maybe he would take his meaty hands, but they would be no good at carefully dissecting muscles and membranes. Would he want his big feet, always covered in black from the polish on his prison boots? They might scare people with their stomping and clattering but what if he wanted to make a stealthy entrance? No, the only thing worth taking from Leo would be his laugh. Then he could keep it hidden if he didn't want it, but if he decided to terrify his victims he could bring it out, loud and coarse and angry. That is the only thing Dismembered Man would take from Leo, but he'd kill him for it all the same, Jonny thought.

I wish I could come and see you this afternoon Ava. You know Mommy used to be in pageants when she was younger, don't you?

Caroline had finished the dress and she came over to where Ava was sitting in front of the make-up table.

Mommy used to dance all night in all sorts of beautiful dresses.

Caroline thought back to the night she'd met Jed in the club. He'd been a big man in those days. A big man from the city. He had money of course, and it didn't really matter where it came from. She didn't even expect him to take her on a second date. And now here she was, dancing with his daughter in the basement.

Mommy let go, you're hurting me. You dance too tight.

Caroline span Ava round in a circle until she squealed.

Again, again.

Now I'm not dancing too tight am I? You're having fun with Mommy?

Ava felt her robe loosen and slip off, the swooshing air against her skin was fresh and she was happy. As she flew through the air she could see the snow spattering the window and she thought of all the fun she could be having outside.

If you're good for Mommy and get ready for the pageant I will make sure there's a sled waiting for you when you get back and I promise Daddy and Leo will take you out and help you build a snowman.

Yay! Okay Mommy you can do my make-up.

First we've got to do your hair, it's shocking young lady, we don't want you going to the pageant with brown roots.

Caroline walked to the sink and took out the powder and bleach cream from underneath to mix in a plastic bowl.

I'd like to come too darling and see you up there in your beautiful new dress, but I can't, I'll be busy at home.

What will you be doing Mommy? Why can't you come?

Oh there's a lot to do. Leo needs clean sheets again and Daddy wants the turkey ready when he gets back so we can have early dinner.

Caroline thought of the dead bird sitting in the kitchen

27

sink, considered how little she wanted to plunge her hands into the pulpy mess of its innards. A man's job really, all that blood and gore. She put on rubber gloves and carried the peroxide paste over to her daughter. The fumes filled their nostrils but they were used to it now. And what was the point of a beauty queen if she wasn't blonde? Caroline used to have beautiful hair. The judges had loved her natural look. She was greying now of course, and paler than she had been, but a few strands still gleamed auburn in the right light. Shame she was always stuck in the basement with the awful violet strip lights. The tiny window was dark but she could tell the weather was getting worse. She hoped Jed and Leo would look after themselves later, she could see no earthly point in going out hunting in this snow. She would say nothing though. Perhaps they'd be too wrapped up in their plans to notice her buying a sled for Ava. What was the harm? It would do her good to have a bit of fun.

Maybe Dismembered Man would get Ava too. Then she wouldn't be so keen on playing dead. The real Dismembered Man could be here in this house already. Ava was always getting so much attention and she wanted to be the doctor as well as the patient. It just wasn't fair. Maybe he could just take her leg or arm and then she wouldn't be beautiful anymore. Or maybe he could take her eyes and then she would have to have fake ones and she couldn't see anymore. Then she wouldn't need his glasses. She was just a stupid baby anyway, she just stood and looked pretty, he would be an important scientist when he was older, a scientist who did very unusual experiments.

Jonny! Ava was calling from down in the basement, Jonny I've got something to tell you.

She's so sweet, he thought, I love her so much. Why was I thinking about cutting her up? He blushed at his meanness and ran down to see her.

What is it Ava? Jonny asked, she looks funny, he thought, with that white paste all over her hair and powder on her face. She looks like a little ghost.

I'm getting a sled for being in the pageant! We can go outside and play on it when we get back. She looked so bright and happy that he almost wanted to stop sulking, but he couldn't help but feel slighted.

Why should you get everything Ava? No one got me anything because I don't stand round looking like a little slut.

Jonny was so mean sometimes, Ava couldn't understand why. She was never mean to anyone; she just wanted him to be nice to her and play with her and to have fun.

Mommy what does that mean? Ava asked? What does standing like a slut mean?

Caroline turned on the tap to wash out Ava's hair and sang *Jingle Bells* as loudly as she could.

24 DECEMBER 1200

Sweet Poisonpie
Appearance: Tiny blood-coloured spores.
Effects: Rose petal flavor with acrid aftertaste. Stomach cramps.
Environment: Damp walls.

An amber glow rose from the valley as the extra generator finally booted up and the streetlights down below came on. The snow had slowed and only a few lone flakes fluttered down on to Daniel's truck as he returned home from his trip to buy new drapes. They were deep red with gold lettering. He thought it looked like Latin but he had never learned it at school, only seen in it in the church hymnals and on the labels of his plants. They were nice and Christmassy, though, made him think of Midnight Mass.

Daniel stopped the car in his driveway and got out. He shifted the heavy material out of the backseat and over his shoulder, slamming the door shut with his free hand. He approached the house quickly, balancing the fabric as best he could whilst he got the keys ready. Daniel leaned heavily against the door expecting it to hold his weight and was taken by surprise when it swung open easily. He let his parcel slide forward on to the floor and steadied himself on the jamb.

Shit! He said as he saw that the drapes were now sitting in the pool of charred paper and water. Pushing the door shut behind him. Daniel picked them up and carried them into the front room. It was better not to think about how stupid he'd been leaving the door unlocked. He wouldn't do it again. He went upstairs to check on the girls. Just in case.

The bedroom was as he had left it, the girls arranged as before. Daniel was so relieved that no one had got in; he began to kiss Magdalena's eyes and Lucy's tiny little pink nose. He would never have been so uncouth as to kiss them on the mouth. When he thought of what had been done to the other three he felt cold. He had scraped so much out of their mouths and genitals. The stench of what he had found was awful. He patted them on the head and let it be at that. He didn't know them like he knew his own girls.

I'm just going down to make the living room more cosy, you can all come down and have a little tea party while I'm out then. It'll be more comfortable.

Daniel went downstairs to hang the new red drapes. He stopped to light another bar on the fire. It was only going to get colder for the rest of the day and he couldn't bear to have to sleep in the freezing cold.

Why can't Mommy come with us to the pageant? Why does she have to cook the turkey for? I don't like turkey anyway I don't like eating birds. It doesn't make sense. Ava was sitting in the back seat of her daddy's car, her hair in tight blonde curls and gold gauze floating out from her body. Her pink lips had been plumped through a mysterious process which the doctor said was completely safe and non-invasive. She didn't like having to sit so still and the dress was getting prickly in the heat from the car heater.

Listen Ava, this isn't a family outing; it's work. You know that. Why do you need Mommy fussing over you all the time? I'm here aren't I? Leo's coming later when he's been to see a man about a dog.

Why has he gone about a dog? What dog?

Well it's not so much a dog as a fox. You know last week

one of these foxes took off a baby when it was sleeping. Something's got to be done.

A fox took a baby? How do you know it was the fox? Did someone see its tail?

Of course it was the fox, you've seen how freaky they've been lately, how big they've got and their teeth are huge.

Ava sat very quietly, thinking about the big teeth. She was only small herself, what if a fox took her?

Daddy?

Yes sweetie?

Why did the fox take the baby? Did it want to look after it?

No I don't think so honey, I think a fox is interested only in one thing, its dinner. That's why we need to kill them all tonight.

Its dinner? You mean he ate the baby?

I wouldn't be surprised if we found a little pile of bloody bones out there somewhere – that's when we know we've got the culprit.

What time should we open today Ginny? Clara, one of the younger dancers in the strip bar was using her friend's real name. She was so bad at remembering to call her Crystal all the time. It was a pretty name, but Ginny was about a lot more than the glass beads on her underwear. It was kind of a house rule that the girls always called each other by their stage names and didn't have personal friendships but fuck that.

It's only twelve thirty Clara, relax. We have all the time in the world. Why don't we have a glass of fizz? It is Christmas. I don't know how many more times I can hear *Jingle Bells* sober.

I'll go and see if Lou wants some, I think she's on the phone to her boyfriend but she's been ages.

They're always on the phone. He's so jealous all the time; I don't think he'll let her do the party tonight. He'll probably want her home putting up her stocking the second the last dance is done. Ginny pulled her superior face and opened the most expensive bottle of champagne, planning to put it on one of the tabs late that night. But not on Jed's or Leo's. Absolutely not.

Oh I can't get Lou off the phone, let's just have some ourselves. Clara had come back with her fox fur from the back room. She was getting colder by the minute and it didn't seem like the snow was going to get any better.

What will the party be like later Ginny? Will it be like the other time? I can't believe how much money they're offering. I don't mind putting on a show but it's not going to be anything too weird is it?

Well you don't make that kind of money easy do you? Don't worry we'll live to tell the tale. I just doubt you'll want to tell it. Ginny knocked back her drink and did her best to look wise and sophisticated. Clara just ate it up.

What time are they coming to see us?

About seven first, they're coming to have a talk with us about the arrangements. If we open about three then we have time to get everything settled and Bob won't suspect anything.

As long as he gets the money rolling into the tills he won't even notice what we're doing or who with.

Exactly.

I'm going to wear something special.

You do that darling. Why the hell not. Ginny did one of her knowing laughs and poured them both another glass.

Merry Christmas Clara, she said, and kissed her on the cheek.

I think I just saw a fox Ava, did you see it go past the car? I think it was going faster than the car. My God it had blood on its mouth.

Jed wasn't a cruel man but he had to stop the kids getting into danger, he couldn't have them eating the mushrooms or going anywhere near those foxes.

Stop it daddy, there wasn't a fox.

There was a fox. It's not safe to be out alone the way these animals are. Do you think they wouldn't eat a little girl like you up? They would.

But why?

I've told you so many times about which mushrooms you're allowed to eat. I saw the mess in the basement. If you or Jonny ate any of the sweet poisonpies you'd better tell me. You know what happens if you eat them?

What? Ava asked with her heart beating funny, she thought of the juice in her mouth.

Well first of all the poisonpie gets into your stomach, then it drips through your blood until at last you can feel it going into your heart. If enough of them get into your heart it bursts and you die.

I die? Ava asked very quietly.

And worst of all, the foxes can smell them on your breath, and the foxes love poisonpies, they love all poison mushrooms because they make the foxes big and strong and dangerous.

Jonny put them in my mouth and I spat them out and I don't want the fox to smell them on my breath and eat me. Oh Oh Oh! Ava began to sob and cry and she didn't care about her stupid gold dress or anything else she just didn't want the fox to eat her.

Listen darling don't be scared, it's okay. I'll look after you. Just stop crying for a minute and let me stop the car. I'll come back there.

Daddy I'm scared of the fox. What if he comes in the car?

I'll shoot him. Jed replied, as he turned the engine off. Then he showed his daughter the shotgun resting across the front passenger seat. Ava stared at the gun. She had seen it lots of times; Leo was always messing about with it. There was one time when Leo took her out in the truck and when they were at the traffic lights he pointed it at her. He said for a joke.

Jed got out of the car and opened the back door. He took a small silver box from inside his pocket and passed it to Ava.

Here, he said, eat some of this pineapple, it will clean out all the poisonpies from your blood.

Really?

Yes I promise. It's magic and it will save you from the fox. It's only daddy's special pineapple that will save you though, so please don't eat any more mushrooms. Just listen to what I tell you and you'll be safe. And if you ever do anything like that again, you come and tell me first. You understand?

Ava put a chunk of pineapple in her mouth and her crying stopped.

Now be a good girl for Daddy and let me straighten you out. Jed leaned into the car and fixed Ava's dress and hair. He took a baby wipe from the makeup case and drew a clean line through each cheek where her mascara had run. He patted white powder over the top and she looked as good as new. He took the metal box back from her and got back into the driver's seat ready to pull away. In the rearview mirror, the glare from the headlights of the car behind illuminated Ava's face to show the two ghostly streaks under the powder on her cheeks.

Daniel began to feel worried, he had tried not to think about it but he knew he had locked the front door. He had been so anxious it was possible he could have made a mistake but he didn't think it was very likely. If that was true then he had to consider the possibility that someone had been in the house. But nothing was missing and the girls hadn't been harmed. If someone had got in they hadn't done anything he could see.

He had finished hanging the drapes and put chairs under all of the doors. He put a pail of water under the letterbox just in case. After making sure the girls were settled in the living room and double locking the doors he went back out to the truck. As he got ready to drive into town he saw something gleam in the hedgerow. Perhaps it was only the glare of headlamps on snow. He drove out on to the road, not registering the tiny bunch of bones, tied with ivy, caught in the dark green of the holly bush.

24 DECEMBER 1300

Vinegar Cup
Appearance: Black. Deep inverted cups hanging from thin stalks. Strong smell of vinegar and thin, runny juice expressed overnight.
Effects: Fatal.
Environment: Bark of dead trees.

Caroline was in the kitchen, her hands inside the turkey. She'd filled the sink with warm water which was slowly turning pink from the bloody insides of the bird. Jonny didn't like turkey – he kept asking questions about what happened to the birds in the sky and why they didn't stay with their families. But Jed was determined he should eat meat, said he would get thin and scrawny if he didn't.

Mom? Jonny asked as he walked into the kitchen. He was still wearing the superman cape wrapped around him, the end trailing along the kitchen floor. Are we going to put up the Christmas decorations?

Caroline thought of all she had to do before Jed and Ava returned home. She turned to look at her son and said that yes of course they could.

Good, Jonny thought, at least they didn't have to wait for Ava to come home. He had thought they would. He was glad because he had an idea he wanted to test out with the fairy lights.

Jonny, I have to get this bird prepared and clean the sheets. We need to go and buy a sled before they get back too. Would you be a darling and help me peel some potatoes? When we get back I promise we'll get on with the decorations. Later, when your daddy gets home you can help him to go and cut down a tree.

I don't want to help him cut down a tree. It's cold and noisy and Leo'll be mean about me.

Well then you don't have to do that but can you please help me peel some potatoes for now? You can come with me and pick out a sled to share with your sister.

Caroline would have liked to say to Jonny that she'd buy him a sled too, but there was no point. After what Jed had said to her earlier she knew he'd never let her buy two. They'd have to share.

Jonny walked over to the kitchen table and sat on the wooden bench near the stove. He removed the superman cape from his shoulders and let it fall into a red heap beside him. The washed potatoes were in a metal bucket on the table and a freshly sharpened knife lay on the chopping board. Jonny began to peel and dice the potatoes and throw them in an empty casserole dish. Caroline had carols on the radio, soft and low.

I hate this song Mom, why do we always have to listen to these Christmas carols?

You know I love the top ten Christmas carols Jonny. I voted for *Silent Night* this year.

Just a lot of annoying little girls singing. Can't you turn it off?

Caroline lifted her hands out of the sink and walked over to the radio. She turned the dial to an untuned void between stations and let the white noise fill the room. She went back to the sink and yanked the bird out of the water, leaving its hollow body drying on some kitchen towel. A violet glob of blood dribbled down the side of the radio. She said nothing more as she cleaned the sink.

Mom, I'm sorry, I know you like the carols. Put them back on. Jonny was surprised at how angry his mother seemed. He didn't know what to do. He peeled another potato in silence.

They're not little girls Jonny; they're young boys who haven't reached puberty. They are extremely talented and they're just about to lose it all.

What? Jonny asked. He didn't know why his mom was so annoyed. The noise felt as though it was getting louder and he couldn't concentrate on the potatoes. Jonny walked to the radio and wiped it with some kitchen towel. He fiddled with the dial until the carols came back on. It was the last verse of *Silent Night*. The announcer advised that it was number two this year, up three places from the year before.

See Mom, it did matter that you voted. You helped it get higher. Jonny said.

You're right Jonny. I did. Caroline said quietly as she basted the turkey. She put it into the oven and came over to help her son finish peeling the potatoes. By the time they were covered with salted water and put into the fridge until suppertime the announcement had been made that *O Holy Night* had won for the third year running.

Damn it! Said Caroline and she turned off the radio for a second time. Let's get out of here. Fuck Leo's sheets. If he wants clean ones he can do his own.

The roads were pretty clear for Christmas Eve. Caroline guessed most people had either gone out already to run their errands or else they were with family already. The snow was coming down in clumps now, feathering over the black ice on the roads. The grit trucks hadn't been out in a while and she wondered whether they had slipped off early, or if they were drinking from hipflasks in their trucks. Either way she'd have to be careful on these roads. She couldn't help thinking of Jed and Leo and how reckless they could be in the truck.

She was still concentrating on the road when Jonny broke the silence.

Mom, look out!

Caroline saw a fox run out in front of the car and she knew if she tried to brake suddenly she might skid. She didn't care about killing the beast but if Jonny saw it he might make a scene. She kept the car at a steady pace and her two hands on the wheel. The fox darted away and she felt a bump, as though she had grazed his back leg.

Jonny thought of the fox, about what would happen to it now. They'd caught her leg and there would be blood matting her fur, perhaps the skin would flake open and reveal bone. It might become infected and lead to gangrene or blood poisoning. Jonny wanted to go after the fox and look at its wounds, maybe bandage them, but his mother would never agree. They arrived at the shops just as they were about to close. The main lights went off like dominoes, leaving only the strings of coloured fairy lights on. The streetlights had gone out again, probably gone on somewhere else. The general store was still open though, the window bright and inviting.

It's so dark Mom, why is it always so dark?

Oh I don't know it's the middle of winter.

As Jonny spoke, the streetlights flickered on again and lit up the row of shops, their red and green window displays glittering in the low light. Jonny felt as though he wanted to be inside the bright shops, not out on the street. Caroline took his arm roughly to cross the street and he didn't squirm away as usual, but softened into her grip.

The general store was deserted. There were no customers or staff to be seen as they jangled the bell on the door and entered. Caroline walked straight over to the display of sleds and began to look at prices.

Jonny saw a really sweet green sled with flames coming all along the length of it. He took his gloves off and ran his hand along the polished sheen of it, imagining how smoothly it would run along the compacted snow. A shop assistant, alerted by the bell, appeared behind Jonny, putting his hand against the wall and leaning in to talk to him quietly, almost in a whisper.

So we've got to convince your mom to buy you this one have we? I can see she's looking at some of the cheaper ones, but we both know that's a false economy.

Jonny did not like the way the man was leaning towards him. He had egg in his beard and two of his teeth were missing. Like Leo, he smelled of whiskey and stale coffee. Jonny stepped away from the sled and walked to his mother's side.

What do you think of this one sweetheart? It's just plain red but it looks solid.

Jonny could see it wasn't nearly as good as the other one but he felt bad about the radio earlier and he hated that the sales assistant thought he could get Jonny to do what he wanted. Looking the man straight in the eye he said to Caroline that he thought it looked good, that he would be delighted to take it and he thought Ava would love it too.

The journey back was difficult, they didn't run across any more foxes but Caroline was worried that they might. The snow had turned to slush and the windscreen wipers were having trouble clearing it away. It was with relief that they returned home and brought the sled into the warm house that smelled deliciously of turkey. They had an hour or two before the pageant was over and decorations to put up.

Jonny wrapped silver tinsel around the banisters whilst Caroline hung their Christmas cards from red cotton on the sitting room wall. Jonny finished quickly and wanted to get the fairy lights to hang outside.

Mom, he shouted, can you give me the key to the attic so I can go and get the fairy lights?

Caroline ignored him so he asked again. Mom, I need to get into the attic.

Caroline came up the stairs towards him, saying that she would go and get the lights. He wasn't to go in the attic. God, she didn't want him going in the attic now.

But you're busy Mom. I don't mind.

Caroline ignored Jonny and bounded up the stairs ahead of him. The keys to all of the rooms in the house hung from a metal loop in her bedroom where Jonny couldn't reach. Jonny knew his mom did not think he knew what was going on in the attic but he did. He had heard noises and crept quietly to the attic door when he was supposed to be asleep.

He took off his shoes and slipped in behind Caroline when she was rummaging for the lights, the room was dark, she was using her torch to see and she didn't notice Jonny in there. He saw the kitten curled up asleep on a pile of blankets. Before Caroline noticed he slipped the warm, sleeping animal into the inside of his jacket and ran down the spiral staircase back to his room. In his room he pulled on wellingtons and a waterproof coat and wrapped the cat in a blanket. He ran out of the back door before his mother had a chance to notice he was gone.

24 DECEMBER 1400

Midnight Bolete
Appearance: Midnight Blue. Small cup with sturdy stalk.
Luminescent Mucus.
Tasteless.
Effects: Hallucinogenic
Environment: Young rosewood

The cars were parked outside the town hall, and the homes were near-deserted as everyone was in the town hall waiting for the pageant to begin. There were even a few visitors from further afield. The Rosewood Beauty Pageant had been a small affair until Ava had gotten famous.

Jed, how are you? We heard you and Ava did well out on the coast. Second wasn't it? Cain Lynch came over and shook Jed's hand as he detached himself from a group of women fussing round his daughter.

First. Jed replied.

First, well I'm sorry if I made a mistake. No need to be difficult about it.

I'm not being difficult at all. I heard Alice came fifth in *Tiny Teardrops*.

She was just recovering from meningitis.

Oh is that what it was. That was what was wrong with her face? Jed did not flinch as he looked his friend in the eye. Then he laughed a little, showed he meant no harm.

Well let's just see Jed, let's just see. Ava's looking a little peaky herself. I heard that she's been burning the candle at both ends.

Not at all Cain, she's feeling perfectly well. She's blooming.

Blooming? Well you don't want her to bloom too much, they get old soon enough.

They do. Jed sounded tired. He pulled a packet of cigarettes out of his top pocket and pointed over to the back of the stage door. Ava was always ready by the time they arrived; Caroline did everything beforehand so Jed didn't have to worry. She was sitting backstage with Ginny and Clara from the Fantasy Bar. They were really good with her, managed to calm her down before she went on stage. Cain's kid was having her hair done by the au pair girl. They might as well step out and have a smoke.

Daniel had arrived at the pageant half an hour before it was due to start, he'd meant to get there earlier but he'd had to go and buy the drapes. It was good to see that people had made an effort. The more people the better for him. He planned to slip away just before the end. He wanted to be safely inside his house before anyone was to drunk. He had a long blue scarf wrapped around the lower part of his face and his coat done up to the top. There was stillness in the air as the people waited patiently for to go inside the hall. The snow was still falling and everyone was muffled and hunched against it. He bowed his head and worried a little about the girls' bare legs in this weather. They were such clever little professionals though; it wasn't easy being crowned Rosewood Christmas Queen.

Daniel could see two men he disliked over the other side of the parking lot, outside the stage door. He didn't know their names but he thought they must be parents. No one else was allowed so close and they sure as shit didn't look like judges. Daniel hated smoking. The amount of flesh wounds he had

to fill and smooth and paint. Even on the girls' faces sometimes. And the worst of it was the smell of the burned material. It never really came out. Once they were wounded, they
lost their sparkle and charm. Daniel didn't care, he loved
them all the same, but he worried sometimes about the kind
of games their partners were playing and how accidental the
burn marks really were. He didn't like the two men because
he had seen them walk past his house and laugh at the
words painted on his walls. They had made the cocksucker
gesture to each other and pointed at Daniel, where he stood
looking out of his own window. The gesture was obscene
and showed the men as crass, overweight idiots. The idea of
these sweet, fragile girls under their care was another worry
to Daniel. If he was looking after one of these girls he would
make sure she was happy. He wouldn't smoke or swear or
let her legs get cold. He checked his watch. Two ten. The
pageant should be starting pretty soon.

Hey Jed, come over here. Leo signalled from inside just as
the first song began and the host arrived onstage, wearing
an obscene amount of fox fur and purple lipstick. Jed saw
him and immediately broke off his conversation with Cain.

See you later Cain, may the best man win. Jed stubbed out
his cigarette and dashed inside the stage door, pushing into
the front row with Leo as the host made her announcements.

Ladies and gentlemen, boys and girls. Merry Christmas
to you all. I hope you all enjoy today. We have a magical
programme lined up for you . . .

Jed ignored the bullshit preliminaries and spoke quietly
into Leo's ear.

Did you get things sorted? Are you ready to come with me
after this?

Yes I can come with you. What are we going to do with
Ava though?

Ava can come with us. She loves the girls, you know that.

But what will Caroline think?

What I tell her to. Jed gave a short laugh.

Leo gave a longer, more raucous one even though his hand shook as he used it to cover his mouth when the laugh turned into a hacking cough.

Jesus Leo, have you even been to sleep? You sound awful.

I was going to, but I went over to see Maria and the kids. It's Christmas Eve.

How did that go?

Okay. I asked if I could go round tomorrow but she said no, said it would upset them too much. I tell you now if I see a silver car in front of the house when I go by to look in the morning, she'll be sorry she never mentioned it to me. Leo's face was red in the cold air but he looked drawn and ill beneath it. Jed punched him gently on the shoulder. Nodded his approval and said nothing more.

There was a wild surge of noise as the girls came out. The front row was almost entirely made up of parents who had good money riding on the contest and they didn't come out in the snow just to stand quietly and watch their daughters get trounced.

Aren't they beautiful? Wendy, an old friend of Caroline's from their pageant days leaned over the back of Jed's seat to whisper in his ear from her position in the second row.

They are Wendy. Almost as beautiful as you and Caroline were.

Oh no, not as beautiful as all that Jed. Wendy laughed and her bad teeth were exposed. Meth, people said.

It was a glitz pageant, the Christmas one, so all the girls had flippers. Jed was glad to look at all those blank even teeth after seeing the mess in Wendy's mouth. A lot of the parents, the moms, were washed up old dishrags; that was why it was better for Caroline to stay home. One man was not a parent; at least he was no part of the circuit that Jed knew about. He was funny looking, hunched over as though he was more scared than cold. He had fluffy ear protectors on like a little girl would wear.

Who is that creep? Jed shouted to Leo over the noise of the crowd.

Oh my god it's that paedo bastard from over the way.

What the guy that got moved to Rosewood a couple of months back?

The same guy. What the fuck is he doing on the front row? He hasn't got any kids, not that he should be allowed kids. You must have heard the stories.

I heard what you told me Leo.

You read the graffiti as well?

Yeah but what does that prove?

It proves that we don't want the fucker hanging round our kids.

Well your kids aren't here so what do you care?

Leo didn't seem to hear Jed as he strode towards Daniel, his fist clenched, as the first individual dance began and a girl of nine showed off her majorette skills whilst wearing a fur bikini and a red Santa hat.

Daniel was having such a wonderful time. The girls were so beautiful. It was true what the hostess said: you could just smell the class in the room. There was absolutely nothing between the majority of the young ladies, not a one of them put a foot wrong. They had strong calves and perfect clear skin, excellent teeth as well. When they flashed their glitzy smiles he just melted, he did. But when Ava came on stage, that was an entirely different matter. It was as though a shower of gold tumbled from heaven all over her. She was dazzling. He held his breath when she came out, his hands clasped as if in prayer. He was so happy, so enchanted that it was too late when the man in the fur-lined cap, with the red face, came over. Daniel saw the mindless violence in his face and tried to stand up, to extricate himself from the crowd, but the man just stood in front of him. The fat woman sitting next to Daniel, wearing bad pearls, spoke to the man in a brusque whisper.

Out of the way Leo, I can't see my little girl with you standing there. You drunk or what?

Daniel took his chance. He jumped out of his chair and walked quickly through the standing people in the aisles. He made his way back to the truck without looking back, and when he finally turned around the man was nowhere to be seen. He was so disappointed to have missed the finale and the winner. When the girls came out together with their beautiful dresses he had been overwhelmed by the colours and the designs. He had certainly not gone away empty handed. He was excited about getting back to his sewing machine and his cosy living room.

I chased the faggot away. Leo said. Jed did not answer; his eyes were fixed on the stage where Ava had just come out to sing. She had a funny, croaky little voice but the coach had shown her how to use it properly. She went all breathy and sexy on the high notes and just belted out the low ones. The backing tape came on and she pouted her way across the stage.

Listen Jed, the cash you get for the pageant.

Shh. I'm listening. Besides, she hasn't won yet.

She always wins. She's a born winner. Anyway, don't go spending that on anything stupid. We need that for tonight, for the club.

I know. Jed looked at his friend for a long time and Leo finally shut up, let him concentrate on the show.

She's a beauty Jed. You're really on to something with her. Leo whistled under his breath. Listen, I'm going to go and wait in the truck, have a smoke. This isn't really my scene.

Fine.

Leo made his way through the crowd, shoulders first, and went to sit in Jed's truck, unlocking it with his master key.

Jed was annoyed with Leo. He was so crass. What was he doing going after that harmless gimp. He enjoyed his sport too much and he never had a thought for the consequences. He was a good man to have on your side but even then, it was a mixed blessing. Jed needed him tonight, no question, but he needed him at least halfway sober and without all sorts of distractions in his head. The other girls came out and did their little performances and then out came the host once more with an announcement. Bad weather meant that the second half of the show would have to be cut short so that everyone could get home safely. That meant that the girls would have to be judged on their first performance only. Safety first and all that. It just so happens that in every pageant ever the girls save their best till last. Their stronger performance would never be seen. Ava, of course, had performed her strongest piece first. Jed went off to have a smoke with Leo before collecting Ava and the prize money.

The money is good in this game Leo. I don't deny it. But I can't hand it over to Ava can I? If she learns that she gets money for parading around then the next thing I know she'll be up there grinding with the strippers for cash as soon as she hits puberty.

No, you're right, that's true. If we keep hold of it and sort of invest it then we can make sure she doesn't get hooked on the money side of it.

All I want is to raise her right. You know morals and standards and a little bit of class. Her mother was a dancer and that had to stop. You cannot be a mother and an exotic dancer.

That you *cannot*. *Cannot*. Echoed Leo. He was barely listening. His shakes had subsided now he knew they had the cash in the bank.

See that's why, Jed started in again, that's why I tell them about the foxes and the poison mushrooms and all, to make sure they don't mess with anything dangerous.

And that's why you don't want them up in the attic too.

Jed stopped smiling, stopped waving his cigarette in the air to make his point.

What did you just say?

Hey, Jed, look they're doing the final procession. We'd better lock up the truck.

24 DECEMBER 1500

Disco Cup
Appearance: Silver, small gelid cup and thick stalk. They grow in patches of hundreds.
Effects: Sedative in small doses, fatal in large doses.
Environment: Swamps and mudflats.

Ginny and Clara stood at the front of the parking lot, cheering as the procession poured out of the hall. This year's new Miss Rosewood was carrying Ava, Miss Baby Rosewood, aloft and both of their crowns glittered under the fairy lights strung across the lot.

Go Ava! Go Ava! Clara cheered.

I think it's disgusting, she said softly to Clara, still smiling across to Ava.

I know. It's hard enough when you get older but this does a child no good. Look at her eyes, they look so sad Ginny.

Well don't get too feeling too sorry for her, she's got a lot more now than we ever had. The money's not bad for a gig like this.

I know that but think about it, how much of it actually goes on her. I mean what do you think she really wants to be doing on Christmas Eve? Most little girls are inside making cards out of glitter or getting mince pies ready for Santa now.

Not all of them, what about the ones standing in front of

us now, looking at Ava and wishing it was them. Besides, before you get too precious about where the money goes, ask yourself how they're paying for the party tonight.

Here she comes; I'll grab her and get her into the car. Jed said he's going to park up at the Fantasy for a while.

Where is Jed? Ginny scanned the crowd as Clara went to follow the procession. Jed was with Bob. Bob handed him an envelope, the prize money. He didn't look too sore which was unusual, if they ever asked for a fair wage he was never so forthcoming. Ginny wondered how he'd feel if he knew his staff would be getting it later and no cut for him. It was a dangerous game for all of them. Jed spotted Ginny and joined her. Together they walked to the car, where Leo had already started the engine. Clara brought Ava to the car and Leo slid over into the passenger seat so all three girls could get in back, Clara and Ginny in their extravagant fox furs and Ava in her gold gauze. The crown sat in her lap and she leaned her head against Clara, drifting off to sleep as the car pulled out. It wasn't far to the Fantasy, but they had to go slow over the black ice.

That faggot's going to be home by now. Leo muttered to Jed. We could pay him a visit.

We've got Ava with us. Jed replied.

Yeah, but I think we should make sure, you know, that he's not nosing round at the club later if you know what I mean? He only lives next door for Christ sakes.

Alright. Jed said. Alright. We can call in. He pushed the shift stick with such force that the car stalled and wouldn't start again.

Daniel was pretty sure they hadn't followed him home. He pulled the car into the driveway and turned off the engine. The streetlamps had come back on again and there was a harsh orange haze around his front door, marking it out in the grey light. For some reason this unsettled Daniel, as though he was under some kind of surveillance. He sat in the car for a moment longer, letting his breathing return to normal. He considered what he had just done, speeding home on the black ice in the near-dark. It upset him that those men could have such an impact on him. He'd been bothered by people like that all his life but it had never driven him to act suicidally before. He had the girls to think about. As his breathing calmed, Daniel felt brave. If only for Lucy's and Magdalena's sake. He got out of the car.

Daniel took off his earmuffs and could hear the car settling down and the buzz of the streetlamp but there was no other sound. One lone crow circled silently above his roof. Daniel walked to his front door and turned the key in the lock and walked in. Shit. He swore. He'd forgotten the bucket of water which was freezing cold and full of shards of ice. His legs were soaking. He kicked it out of the way and listened very carefully. There was nothing but the hiss of the radiator in the hallway. He locked the door top and bottom and fastened the chain. He went into the downstairs toilet and grabbed a towel from the rail. He mopped at the water with it and then rolled it in a sausage shape to stuff under the door. Once he was satisfied with this he went to the back door, checked it was locked and put a chair under the handle. Finally, he peeked into the living room to check that the ladies were okay. Only after he had done all of these things did Daniel go and change into some dry clothes.

Jonny was cold and the kitten was crying. She didn't like being stuck inside Jonny's jacket. He had been sitting up in his old tree house for more than an hour. He was watching for the car to see when his sister got back. Then he planned to run home and show her the kitten, to spoil the surprise his parents were hiding from her. He was sick of Ava getting all the good presents when he got nothing. It was so cold up in the tree though, the branches were bare and snow was blowing through the gaps in the tree. Jonny had put his coat on but he'd forgotten his gloves. The kitten was warm against him but she kept giving out piercing little cries and he felt bad.

Daniel had built this tree house two years ago with his father. That had been back when the house had been abandoned and the garden was anyone's. The good thing about this tree was that it looked across the valley; you could see what was going on for miles around. You could see into the house as well, and the shed where the man Daniel seemed to spend a lot of time. Jonny could see the words spray-painted on the side of the shed too. 'Nonce', 'Queer' 'Cunt'. The words had been covered over in white paint but they showed through. The streetlight sparkled on the pristine wall and the white paint was like a sheer film over the tall, red letters. Jonny had seem the men who'd done it, and they were his friends' fathers, even though he'd heard them blame their sons. Leo had been there too, but not his father. Jonny didn't know why they hated Daniel so much. Jonny had wanted to ask him about the experiments he did in the shed. He'd seen the shadows behind the drapes. But he was too shy and thought it would get him in some sort of trouble. He was distracted by the kitten's mewing.

Don't worry puss, he said, I'm not going to stay here forever, I'm hungry and I doubt you'd fill me up.

The cat didn't seem to care whether Jonny ate her or not, she was scared of him either way. He didn't have his torch with him and if they didn't hurry up it might be difficult for him to make his way down the rope ladder in the dark. He'd expected his mom to call for him a while back but he hadn't seen her leave the house. She didn't seem to care too much about Jonny or the kitten. He thought they couldn't be much longer, but he wasn't sure. Sometimes they took a really long time but his mom had said they were having early dinner; that was why she was making such a fuss about the turkey.

The kitten must have been too tired to carry on making a noise because she had fallen asleep and her jumpy little heart had become regular, in time with Jonny's. He decided to give it ten more minutes and if they hadn't come he would make his way back home.

Jonny wrapped himself tighter in his coat and searched through the tree house for a set of binoculars so he could recognise his dad's car. He found them, they were bright blue and plastic but they worked pretty well. He turned back to the opening of the hut and used the binoculars to look into the distance. He could see the main road to the town sprinkled with Christmas lights. He judged the time to be about right to make his way home.

Jonny began to make his way down, careful with his footing on the frozen rope. He made slow progress, left foot, right hand, right foot, left hand. The kitten had woken up and was squeaking and wriggling inside his coat. When he was about halfway down he got scared, really scared, that she was going to jump out. Instinctively, he grabbed her with both hands, and fell backwards; he managed to get both feet caught in the rope as though it were a pair of stirrups but his momentum carried him down. To avoid being dashed into the tree trunk he let both feet slip through the rope and landed head first on the snowy lawn, the yowling kitten still inside his jacket.

Daniel had his scrapbooks out in the living room. He'd managed to get a couple of Polaroids before being noticed on the front row. He showed them to the girls and saw how excited they were by what he'd captured. In his scrapbooks he had all of his design ideas for new outfits and hairstyles and makeup. He would never, never abandon his girls but he would have loved a job on the pageants. He loved the grace of the little girls, their perfect beauty. In the centre pages of one of his best scrap books he had recreated the Rosewood Summer Pageant. It was a big one, the biggest around here. He'd known about it long before he'd set foot in this cold valley. He had all the clippings from magazines pasted in to his books. Ava had won the last two years, the first time she had been four years old. It wasn't allowed of course, but the judges slipped her through on some technicality. Or lie perhaps. He'd been following her career for a long time. Daniel took out his craft knife and cut up the Polaroids. He cut each girl out separately and stuck them on to the stage he had drawn. He knew that they were wearing different clothes then, it had been an under-the-sea theme in blue and green, but it didn't matter. They looked stunning in their Christmas dresses and he knew exactly where to place them. It was so sad that he hadn't seen Ava receive her crown, as surely she would have done, and he stuck her on last, at the centre, her blond ringlets being blown by the wind. He left the scrapbook to dry by the fire and sat back to take a sip of his hot whiskey. He felt better already.

Daniel walked to the kitchen to put the kettle on for a second hot toddy. He could hear a muted slow thudding from the front garden and pulled the blind aside to see what was going on. The rope ladder had swing free from the big tree at the bottom of the garden and the wooden rungs were slapping into the trunk as they were flung by the wind. He'd been meaning to pull it down for a while, he was sure some of the kids climbed up there sometimes. Daniel put his boots and coat back on and walked out into the garden. He could hear something else as he came nearer to the tree. It sounded like a cat crying. He felt a sickening chill as he thought of the foxes. What if one of them had injured a smaller animal and lay in wait for him now? He hesitated a moment but considered that the cat might die if he left it. He continued to the tree.

Jonny's sight was a little blurred when he came round. He couldn't work out where he was but there was a lot of white on the edge of his vision. His hands were tingling and he couldn't make them move. His head was painful and heavy and he decided to stay where he was for a minute while he caught his breath. He was surprised to find himself sitting up suddenly. It almost felt as though someone had dragged him.

A pain ran through his shoulder and he slumped back down.

You've hurt yourself. You must be freezing, let me bring you inside and get you warm. I'll give the kitten some warm milk.

What? Jonny asked? He could see the face of the strange man looking down at him. He remembered what he had been doing. The tree house.

Where is she? The kitten? Jonny panicked.

She's here in my cardigan. She's fine. I don't think she knew quite what was going on!

Jonny started shivering violently. The man took off his overcoat and wrapped it round Jonny. He fished in the pocket and brought out his earmuffs which he placed on Jonny's head.

Come on, you're freezing, let's go inside.

Jonny hesitated, even in his confusion he thought of the words on the side of the shed. He remembered the stories about kids who went with strange men and came back as parcels of meat. But he was so cold and wet and sore. It wasn't completely dark yet so he couldn't have been on the ground for long. Not long enough for anyone to come looking. Before he could answer, Jonny heard the sound of a car driving really fast and bright white lights lit up the snow.

Fucking Faggot! Jonny heard Leo before he saw him. What are you doing with the kid? Jonny could see Leo's boots walking towards him; he moved his head a little and could see his father right behind.

Jonny are you okay? His father asked.

Fine, Dad, fine.

He fell down from the tree house, I think. He's very cold. If you would all like to come inside and have a hot drink? Daniel spoke softly to the two big men.

Daniel knew there was nothing good could come of this. He should have left him there in the snow. But the kitten didn't deserve anything bad to happen to her. He thought that if he

57

was as gentle as possible they might leave him alone. He was only trying to help the boy. He couldn't help looking over to the car though, past their heads and into the backseat where Ava sat in her gold dress, she was like a Christmas angel. Two whores were in the back with her. Daniel had seen them at the parade. One of the men picked the boy up and carried him to the car, still wearing the coat and the earmuffs. Daniel was too scared to ask for them back. The other man stood in front of him, saying nothing.

This is the kitten. Do you want to take her? He asked the silent man.

What you doing with the kitten that's her Christmas present. You fucking prick, you've ruined it for her. The man looked genuinely disgusted and there was nothing Daniel could say to explain himself. The man took the kitten from him and brought it back to the car. Daniel stood shivering and coatless in his front garden and watched as the car pulled away and sped off down the road.

24 DECEMBER 1600

Destroying Angel
Appearance: Blue caps, thick grey stems.
Effects: Anaphylactic shock.
Environment: Radioactive locations.

Jed had dropped the girls back at the club before driving home.

Leo, can you do me a favour and bring Jonny and the kitten inside before Ava wakes up? I'll follow you in with Ava in a minute. There's nothing much we can do about this now. Jed spoke with authority and though Leo muttered under his breath, he did as Jed asked.

I'm fine, Jonny said and pushed Leo off. Jed watched them walk in, Jonny with his red earmuffs and Leo with a kitten in his arms. It was not what they had planned. Thank Christ they'd driven past the old queer's when they had and seen what he was doing. Just meant they'd have to put their plans back a bit.

What happened? Jonny's mum asked. She didn't look surprised to see him bundled up in a stranger's coat with a bruise on his head.

Mum, you didn't come and look for me. Jonny said. He felt like he was going to cry but he didn't want to. He took the stupid earmuffs off and threw them on the floor.

Why did you take the kitten? She asked as she took her from Leo. Come on, upstairs both of you. She said, without giving him a hug.

Jonny was warmer now and he could feel the pain in his shoulder. He didn't really understand what had happened with the strange man, but he was glad to be back in his own house now, away from him. Jonny followed his mum up the stairs and saw that she was taking the kitten right up to the top of the house and the attic. He followed her to check that the kitten would be okay. He did feel responsible.

Get into your room, his mum said, what are you following me for?

I just wanted to check she was okay.

You know you're not meant to come into the attic, all your presents are in here.

Sorry Mum. Jonny said and made his way into his room. He took off the old man's coat and then his own coat.

Jonny, his mum called, I'm running you a bath.

Okay Mum. He shouted. He took all of his clothes off and put on his fluffy blue bathrobe. He lifted up his pillow and took out the Spiderman pyjamas he'd got last Christmas. He wasn't that bothered about Spiderman anymore but he loved how comfy they were. He walked across the hall to the bathroom.

Caroline had made sure the animal was warm in the attic. She'd given her some kitten milk and put her near the radiator. When she'd locked the door, the exhausted creature had fallen asleep. Caroline was running the bath for Jonny now, he looked frozen solid. She didn't have time for all of this nonsense. He came in, looking pathetic.

Get in then, I've put your favourite Captain Bubble in. She softened when she saw how sad he looked.

Jonny dipped one toe in to check the temperature and wiggled it gingerly. Caroline was frustrated, the temperature was fine, she'd checked it herself. She picked her son up by the shoulders and dunked him under the water. By the time he emerged from the water, he had a foam beard. She laughed at how silly he looked and he joined in.

Now let's see what's dirt and what's hurt, Caroline said, tenderly sponging Jonny's body as she looked for bruises.

Ava was back in the basement. She didn't remember getting home and she didn't know what had happened to Aunty Clara and Aunty Ginny. Her daddy had carried her inside and she'd woken up because she could feel his chin tickling her and she could hear Leo's voice. At first she'd got scared in case it was Leo carrying her, she hated him touching her. But it was her daddy, she could tell by the smell. And his chin wasn't nearly as prickly as Leo's. Daddy had told her that Mummy was giving Jonny a bath and that she should go and take her make-up off. He promised that they could go out on the sled if she was a good girl. She wanted to go on the sled so badly. It was dark now and it wasn't as good. She took off her dress and hung it up carefully. Her jeans and red pullover were icy cold but she knew they'd warm up soon. She put on her fluffy pink slippers and started to warm up again. Ava sat at her dressing table and began to smooth off the make-up with cotton wool and cream like Mummy had shown her. She was done in five minutes and ran all the way upstairs to the warm stove in the kitchen where her daddy and Leo were talking.

The kitchen was empty when Ava got there. The coffee pot was on the stove but the two men had disappeared. Ava saw that her mummy had left out the glitter and glue so they could make cards together. Ava could not decide what to do. She really wanted to go on the sled but she wanted to make cards as well.

Jonny and their mummy came into the kitchen. Jonny had a funny purple mark on his head and his hair was damp and fluffy.

Come on you two, their mummy said, sit down and make some Christmas cards. We need to bring them to church tomorrow so get busy.

But what about the sled? Ava asked.

Daddy will take you out soon. Come on now, cards please Madam.

Ava took a seat next to the stove and patted the wooden bench beside her. Come on Jonny, come and help me. I've missed you.

I missed you too Ava.

What happened to your head Jonny? Ava asked.

I decorated it for Christmas. He replied. But Ava didn't think that made sense.

They had to make six cards. One for the priest and one for Leo's family. One for the Bartons and one for Mr. Connell who ran the pageants. Two for some old ladies Ava didn't like because they smelled funny and always asked her if she'd said her prayers.

Can I make one for Auntie Clara? Ava asked. She thought about making a big glittery peacock for her, because she had shown Ava a picture of the bird in a book. Mummy did not seem to hear and she had only left enough pieces of card to do the six. Ava thought she could make her one another time. She just wanted to get this done and get out on her sled. Jonny seemed to think the same, they made the cards in about fifteen minutes, and were just leaving them next to the stove to dry, when their daddy came into the kitchen.

Hey kids how're you doing? He said.

Ava showed him the cards she'd made.

They're beautiful sweetie. He'd said.

How'd you like a special treat? Leo got these earlier from the market. Why don't you try one?

He held out a paper bag. Jonny pulled a face. He seemed in a funny mood. No I don't want one, I know what they are.

Ava could see something sparkling in the bag; there were lots of round, white balls inside with frosted sugar coating. They smelled like vanilla. She out her hand in the bag and took one. She ate it in one gulp.

Good girl. Her daddy said. Do you want to go out on the

sled now?

Ava squealed and grabbed his hand.

Jonny said to his father, I'll just go and get dressed, wait a minute.

No, you've had enough excitement for one day son. You stay in those warm clothes and sit by the stove until dinner. I'm only going to take her out for a few minutes to stop her moaning. She deserves it after the money she's made today.

Their dad left the room to help Ava on with her snowsuit.

Jonny looked out of the window, he could see where his dad and Leo had left their spades after they were digging this morning. Ava stepped out in her white snowsuit and he saw their dad carry out the red sled. He gave Ava a push down the hill and she sped off, he ran down to meet her at the bottom with his torch because the light from the house would not reach all that way. Jonny wondered what they would think if the lights were off by the time they got back. He flicked the kitchen light switch and the square patch in front of the house turned grey, the spades frozen into the grounds like alien stalagmites.

Jonny took a sharp knife from the kitchen drawer and brought the bag over to the light of the stove. He split open one of the sweets from the paper bag and blood gushed out onto the cards, mingling with the gold glitter. Jonny peeled the frosted coating from a second sweet and saw what he expected to find. Leo had bought these sweets before and handed them round to the men with him at the strange old man's house the day they'd written words on his shed. Bullseyes he'd called them, and that's what they were. Beneath the sticky surface was a complete eye, yellowy and bloodshot, the pupil glazed and dead. Jonny laughed when he thought of the trick his dad had played on Ava. It served her right.

24 DECEMBER 1700

Alpine Brittlegill
Appearance: Green lichen
Effects: Synaesthesia
Environment: Pine forests

What's your brother gone and switched the light out for? Jed said, but without expecting Ava to respond. She was laughing and breathless from sledding down the hill. Jed shone his torch in front of him but it didn't give him enough visibility.

Listen sweetie, you stay here and wait for Daddy. I've got to go into the house and switch the light on. I don't want to drag you up in the dark. I'll only be a minute.

Jed turned and walked to the house before Ava had a chance to whine. He was pissed off with Jonny, he never did anything right. He was too much of a dreamer always going on about aliens and experiments. Well maybe Leo was right, if school didn't toughen him up they'd have to do something about it themselves. It didn't help either that he spent so much time playing with Ava, he had to admit Leo had a point there. But it was none of his damn business what Jed did with his kids. It wasn't like Leo had done so well himself. The battery on the torch was going, but Jed could make out the house just ahead. He could see the spades, frozen where they'd left them. That'd be another job, getting them out of the earth again, he thought as he covered the last stretch.

Ava sat as still and quiet as she could in the sled. Her daddy had disappeared too quickly for her to tell him she was scared. It had been fun in the sled, for the first time the day had felt like Christmas. It had been good getting the crown but she had so many now. But now, she was scared to be alone in the sled, she thought of the foxes that might be around. Her daddy had told her that eating the red mushrooms made the foxes able to smell her. She kept her mouth closed tight and tried not to breathe until he came back. She could hear the noise of a crow, it made her worried. It wasn't a nice noise and she wondered if a crow might want to eat her too. At last, the kitchen light came on and she could see her daddy walking towards her. He looked funny, like he was angry. Ava wanted to go inside, she was sick of being out in the cold. When her daddy came back and started pulling her uphill, she was glad that the sledding was over.

Caroline came down to the kitchen and picked up the Christmas cards to be handed out in church the next morning. She did not notice the blood; she thought it was red glitter. She stood the cards up on the dresser amongst the ones the family had received. Jonny had disappeared and so had Leo. The door opened and Jed dragged Ava all the way into the kitchen in her sled, leaving a trail of wet, grimy slush on the polished tiles.

Did you enjoy yourself Ava baby? Caroline asked her daughter.

It was alright but I'm cold now. Ava replied.

What's up with her? Caroline asked her husband, she doesn't look too good.

She has too much, that's her problem, she doesn't know how lucky she is to get a present like this, and a day before Christmas as well.

Okay. Caroline said quietly as she began to peel Ava out of her wet snowsuit.

Come on Ava, bedtime. I'll read you a story and you can go straight to sleep to wait for Santa.

Okay. Ava said, shivering in her underwear.

I'm just going to bring your wet things down to the basement to wash and then I'll bring you upstairs. Caroline took the pile of clothes and took them to the cold, stone steps which led from the kitchen to the cellar. She pulled the light on and waited on the top step for the basement to become visible. Once it was safe, Caroline continued down the stairs, passing the red-splattered window on the way and thinking she would come and clean it once Ava was settled. The big metal table they used for butchering game was also spattered with mushrooms from where Ava had dribbled them out. She would have to clean that too, didn't want it getting into the fox meat.

Caroline walked underneath the length of the house and reached the utility room. Steam lay heavy on the air as hot water swirled through the washing machine. She went to the dirty laundry basket and was about to dump Ava's clothes in when she noticed something she didn't recognized in there. Jed and Leo's clothes were filthy from the night before, but in amongst their bloody shirts, was a silver sequined evening dress. Not hers and not Ava's. There was blood on that too, soaking the shoulder. Much more than would have come off their clothes. Caroline dropped Ava's clothes on the floor and took the dress from the basket. Then she placed Ava's clothes on top of the shirts.

Caroline walked quickly back to the metal table at the other end of the basement, holding the dress and grabbing a pair of scissors from her sewing kit as she went. At the table she cut the bloody portion of the dress off. She opened the freezer and took out a joint of meat wrapped in muslin. Wrapping the piece of fabric tightly around the fox meat she replaced it in the freezer. The rest of the dress she cut into scraps. She walked back to her sewing kit and put the scissors back, the silver material she bundled in with all her other fabrics. Finally, she washed her hands at the small sink by Ava's dressing table, and made her way back upstairs.

Ava was alone in the kitchen. She was standing in front of the stove, but she was still in her underwear. Caroline picked her up and gave her a cuddle.

Come on smelly, let's get you to bed.

Ava didn't smile or hug her back. She hung limp in Caroline's arms and made a soft moaning sound. Caroline tickled her as they climbed up the stairs. Ava wriggled and began to laugh. They got to Ava's room and Caroline threw her up in the air and caught her over the bed.

Again Mummy! Ava said, her sullenness forgotten. Again! Again!

Caroline threw her higher and finally let her bounce off the bed. Ava giggled and burrowed down amongst her bedclothes. Caroline turned the radiator higher because Ava felt so cold. She opened Ava's top drawer to take out her nightclothes and looked out of the window before she shut the curtains. She couldn't see Jed or Leo. She knew better than to ask questions, but she thought it was pretty obvious something was going on. Leo had said he was going to check on Maria and the kids. She'd better give Maria a call to warn her in case her new man was planning on staying.

Here you go Ava, let's get you into these warm pajamas. Caroline helped her daughter on with the pajamas even though Ava was quite capable of getting into extravagant dresses by herself and even doing her own makeup.

Mummy, Ava said, I'm scared of the foxes. I don't want you to turn the light off.

How will the foxes get in here?

Because if Santa comes down the chimney and reindeers can come into my room, maybe foxes can.

Don't be silly Ava. I'll turn your nightlight on but no foxes are going to come and eat you.

Will you read me a story Mummy?

Of course, now snuggle down and I'll read.

Ava settled under the covers, worried still about the foxes and Santa, but looking forward to the story. Her mummy began to read.

The wicked queen turned to the dark-haired boy and sent him to do her evil bidding. She sent a black raven with him to frighten anyone who tried to escape from the forest.

Ava said. What's a raven?

A big, black bird, her mummy told her.

Like crow?

No, much bigger. Don't worry about crow.

The blonde-haired girl was wearing frilly lace dress covered in pink roses. The evil boy took a knife from his pocket and plunged it into her dress where her heart would be. It cut so deep and so cold that no blood came out of the wound, instead the knife froze into place inside her. Her screams died on the breeze and the only sounds in the forest were the boy's cruel laughter and the caw-caw-caw of the raven.

Ava didn't like the story so she pretended to be asleep. Her mummy closed the book and put it down. She turned the big light off, but left the starlight on. Ava saw her look out of the window once more before shutting the curtains tight, tucking the bottoms into the radiator, and leaving the room. She did not look back at Ava before she went.

24 DECEMBER 1800

Slime Cap

Appearance: Brown layered fungus, erratic sizes, covers young trees in sheets. Slimy coating which is sticky to the touch.

Effects: Kills young plants and shoots. Cause vomiting in animals and nausea in humans.

Environment: Near young trees and plants.

Jonny had been upstairs thinking about how to get into the attic. He wanted to go and play with the kitten again. They'd had quite an adventure together and he wanted to check she wasn't mad at him. But his stupid parents wouldn't let them go in there. That was why it was perfect for hiding things. Their dad had told them it was dangerous to go in there because of the electrical equipment and the boilers. But Jonny didn't think they could be that dangerous or his mum wouldn't go in. It was just a lie so they could hide their birthday and Christmas presents. Jonny really wanted to go in and see the kitten though so he decided to behave during dinner and then pretend to be busy in his room. He had seen his mum leave the keys in her bedroom and if he was careful he could bring the chair over to the bed and take the keys. He knew how bad it would be if he got caught but he didn't really care today. Everything had been awful. It was the worst Christmas ever.

Caroline was tired. She wasn't looking forward to this meal. The men would be going out straight afterwards and she didn't care what they were going to do. She just wanted some peace. She turned the steamer on and let the vegetables cook for a few minutes while she made the bread sauce.

Jonny! She called, Can you come and set the table?

Jonny came downstairs as soon as he heard his mum's voice, he had decided to be very, very good.

Jonny took knives and forks from the drawer and laid them out. He opened the low cupboard in the dresser and removed five water glasses.

No Jonny, we only need four glasses.

Isn't Leo eating with us? Jonny was thrilled to hear this; the sight of Leo sucking on a leg bone was more than he could bear. It really put him off his dinner.

No, Ava's not. She's gone to bed. She's too tired.

Jonny felt bad again. He knew she would have been scared when he turned the lights off. He decided to bring her up something when he'd set the table. He set a jug of iced water in the middle of the table along with salt, pepper, vinegar and oil. His mum passed him a bowl of salad and he set that down too.

We'll let your dad carve the turkey, she said. I'm putting the plates in to warm now so can you please go and fetch him and Leo. I think they're doing something to the car.

Sure. Jonny said. His mind was elsewhere. He opened the fridge and took out a dish of pineapple. He took a spoon from the drawer and brought it upstairs to his sister. Jonny knocked on the door but she didn't say anything. He walked into the room and saw her curled up on her side, facing the wall. He put down the pineapple beside the bed and left it there, in case she got hungry later. Then he ran downstairs and out to the front to tell his dad and Leo that dinner was ready.

Caroline put the potatoes and peas on four hot plates, then she set out them on the table with the jug of bread sauce. The men came in, with Jonny, streaking filth on the floor.

Can you put your dirty boots over in that corner with the sled please? I'll do the floor when you're out but I don't see why you have to make so much extra work for me.

Hear that Jed? said Leo. We need to leave our boots tidy for your wife. He walked all the way across the floor, removing his boots only when he reached the far side, and then he threw them on top of the sled, mud and oil splattering the seat. Jed removed his boots carefully and walked over to the sled. He placed them on the newspaper Caroline had left underneath the sled and pulled Leo's out, placing them next to his. He walked in his stockinged feet over to the sink and washed his hands. Leo looked at him and raised an eyebrow, chuckling low.

That's it Jed, you play nice. You're just a good boy deep down. You want to be careful you don't turn into a faggot too.

Caroline set the turkey platter down heavily on the table and the thump stopped Leo's conversation.

Leo, would you mind carving? She said.

I wouldn't mind at all Caro, he said.

Then I would appreciate if you washed your hands first. She replied.

With a lot of splashing and grunting, Leo washed his hands and stood at the head of the table to carve.

Caroline put a Christmas record on at a low volume. She took her place at the table, bent her head and put her hands together.

We'll say grace first. She said. Bless us oh heavenly father and thank you for these thy gifts. Thank you for the turkey who wanders the earth and thank you for the potatoes that grow in the ground, and thank you for our family and friends.

Leo had already begun to carve the turkey with the electric knife. Caroline raised her voice above the sound of the machine.

Thank you for blessing our family with at such riches and please keep all of us safe from the harm that men do against your will. Amen

Amen, said Jonny

Amen, said Jed.

I'm fucking starving, said Leo.

Poor Leo, thought Caroline, he doesn't know how to behave. She was glad she'd called Maria, he was hungover, drunk and angry all at once. She wished they could move him on, somewhere else. Somewhere far away from her family. But that was going to be a long wait. She poked at the dark meat and ate some salad. By the time she'd finished her tomatoes the men had swallowed down nearly half a bird. Pigs, she thought, dirty pigs. She tried not to meet Leo's bloodshot eyes from across the table. She knew what that meant and she was not in the mood tonight.

Jonny, his dad said, why don't you go up and read in bed. Leo and me have to go out and see a man about a dog, and your mother's got the Christmas presents to see to. Maybe it's best you have an early night.

Sure, Jonny said. I want to finish Dismembered Man anyway. He'd finished it several times over and was reading it for the seventh time but he didn't necessarily want them to know that. He cleared his plate and kissed his mum on the cheek. His dad reached across and ruffled his hair. Leo gave him a nod. Jonny walked upstairs, and banged his bedroom door shut. He switched his reading light on and pulled the curtains so if anyone looked from outside it would seem as though he was in there. He took off his slippers and walked as quietly as he could back across the room. He had thought about the best way to get the keys from their hook and he decided the best thing to do was to stand a chair on the bed. It wouldn't be easy but if he fell it would be on to the soft mattress. He opened his door a crack and slid his whole body around the tiny pocket of space he had created. There was almost no noise. Very slowly and carefully he walked across the landing, and peered through the rails at the top of the stairs to check what the adults were doing. They hadn't moved from the table, even though they'd said they were going to. They were talking too softly for Jonny to hear but they were busy for the moment.

Jonny walked over to his parents' bedroom slowly and carefully as before and was happy to see the bedroom door open. He didn't want to make a creak. The room was lit by moonlight and he could see the keys hanging on the hook above the bed. He knew that they were just too high for him to reach, he'd tried before. But he'd never been so desperate to get into the attic. Jonny looked at the chair under his mother's dressing table and wondered how he could manage to drag it over the bed without making a sound. His parents' bedroom was over the sitting room and he knew they were in the kitchen. He was standing in the doorway, thinking about how to do it, when he heard footsteps on the stairs. He was glad he hadn't turned the light on but he didn't know what he could say to explain what he was doing if someone came in. he crouched down and waited behind the door, making himself as small and still as possible. He waited, and no one came. He thought he must have been wrong and imagined the steps. After a few minutes, he thought there was no way anyone could be upstairs, but he was too anxious to move the chair. He padded out of the room on all fours and made his way back across the landing to the top of the stairs.

I don't hold with killing for no reason, his mummy said quite loudly.

Keep your voice down, his daddy said but just as loudly, It doesn't do to have these foxes running wild, you know that as well as I do Caro.

Jonny could see all three of them sitting at the table, their dirty plates in front of them. He wondered why they'd sent him to bed and said they were so busy. They didn't seem busy. It didn't look like they'd moved either, he wondered if Leo had been trying to scare him by pretending to come upstairs.

But I can't stand taking the kids through that terrible smoke. Every time you go out and cull the foxes you leave their flesh and bones burning all over the valley.

You don't complain of the extra meat, said Leo, even if they are pure vermin.

The fur as well, that's worth something, said his daddy.

Had to be done anyway, I wouldn't want little Ava seeing her new pet kitten mauled by foxes. It doesn't do to have these beasts roaming around.

No it doesn't do to have beasts roaming. It certainly doesn't Jed. Leo said and slammed his coffee mug on the table. He stood up and walked to the far end of the table where Jonny's mummy sat. He put his hands on her shoulders and started to rub them from behind. Jonny felt funny, he wasn't sure if he liked Leo touching his mummy. He wondered why she didn't tell him to stop. Then Leo leaned around and kissed her on the mouth, Jonny's daddy hadn't moved and he didn't say anything. Leo moved his head away and wiped his mouth with the back of his hand. He walked away from the table to the part of the room that Jonny couldn't see from the top of the stairs. Jonny's mummy looked up then, right to the spot where Jonny was standing. She gave him a funny smile and then looked away. Jonny ran back into his room, not worrying anymore about making a noise. He threw himself under the blankets and curled up pretending to be asleep in case anyone came upstairs. The light was bothering him but just for that minute he couldn't get up to turn it off. He decided it was better to stay where he was and shut his eyes as tight as possible.

24 DECEMBER 1900

Cramp Balls
Appearance: Cream-coloured mushrooms. Soft puffballs.
Effects: Harmless and edible (misnomer) delicate and fla-
voursome.
Environment: Snow, frost and wetlands.

Caroline was standing at the kitchen window finishing the
dishes. The orange haze from the streetlight looked beautiful. It was softened by condensation and mist. She thought it
would be nice to look at the warm light for a while, just standing with her hands in the hot bubbles, they felt so clean. She
sighed. There was no time for that. The men had left only ten
minutes ago, but they'd had time to get to Maria's. Caroline
knew that she had her new man staying, she'd wanted him to
be there for the kids on Christmas morning. She'd told Leo he
could come for Christmas lunch at one. Billy, her boyfriend,
would walk them to church then meet up with his mother
and part company with them. He and Leo didn't have any
cause to meet. But Maria was human, she was in love with
Billy, she said, she had colour now, she was alive. Leo was
nothing if not skilled at detecting changes in the moods of his
wife and children. They were doing so well without him, he'd
asked around. He was having a fling with the hairdresser's
assistant, he got the car registration from her, all she'd had
to do was take it down when Billy dropped Maria off for her

appointments. And with a car registration number, and a big computer at the prison, there was quite a lot he could do.

Caroline thought it was unlikely they'd return now, so she drained the sink, dried her hands right up to the elbow on a dishcloth and walked out to the hallway. She picked up the receiver of the telephone and dialled Maria's number. It rang ten times, twenty times and there was no answer. Caroline put the phone down and thought of the possibilities. Billy might have taken them out somewhere for a treat, or they could be playing in the snow. But it was dark and cold and a mist had been developing. They wouldn't take the kids out in that. It wasn't safe. Caroline lifted the receiver again and pressed redial. Then she stopped herself. What if she'd dialed the wrong number? She opened her phone book and redialed carefully. There was still no answer. Ten rings, twenty, thirty. And then Caroline was worried because she couldn't understand why the answer machine didn't click in. it suggested that the phone was unplugged or somehow diverted. She decided to call the operator just in case.

You drive for a bit Leo, Jed said. He was so tired now that he couldn't see in front of him even without the mist.

You drive and I'll look out the, out the . . . the . . . window. I'll see what I can see. Jed yawned and felt his grip on the steering wheel go limp.

Pull over then Jed. I'm not going to sit on your faggot lap.

Jed couldn't tell what was coming, but he felt pretty sure he was safe to pull over for a minute. He braked slowly and though he knew he should get out straight away he couldn't. He sat there for just a second and stared at the mist. He just let it come right at him.

Jed, you getting out or what? Leo poked his friend and sounded almost concerned. Jed shivered and banged the driver's door open so it wrenched on the hinge. He stepped out of the car, leaving the engine running. Leo came round, let him pass, and then took the driver's seat. As soon as Jed switched into the passenger side, Leo set off at a pace, barely waiting for the door to shut.

Jed used his sleeve to wipe a hole in the condensation and kept up his part of the bargain. Looking out of the window. Seeing what was coming.

We'll hear them before we see them anyway. Jed said

Not at the speed we're going. Leo said.

Jed cranked open the window just a slit. There was a cracking sound as he broke the layer of ice that had begun to form. It was still mostly wet, and dripped down his arm. It felt good though, it woke him up.

Can you shut the fucking window?

We need to be able to hear the foxes, and besides, it's keeping me awake.

Yeah? This'll keep you awake. Leo accelerated the car and drove until they reached the fork. Instead of going to the left, to the strip club, he turned right. Towards his old house.

Leo, are you still drunk? You took the wrong turning.

Have you got the gun down there?

You know I have, what else are we going to kill the foxes with?

Ok. Good.

Leo said nothing and Jed could feel the wheels spinning beneath them, getting no traction on the black ice. He didn't feel too much like distracting Leo or arguing with Leo so he buckled his belt and went along for the ride.

Here. Leo eventually said. I'll walk from here. And he braked at the foot of a hill. Don't turn the engine off; it'll never get going again. Leo reached down to Jed's feet and took the shotgun. He straightened up, opened the car door and stepped out. Jed watched him climb the hill on foot, using the loaded gun as a staff.

Mum, asked Jonny, can I go and see the kitten now Ava's asleep? He had come downstairs once he knew that Jed and Leo had gone.

77

Caroline was on the phone to the operator, waiting for the woman to get back to her on the problem with Maria's phone.

Shh. She said to Jonny.

But I think she might be lonely up there.

She won't be lonely. Just forget about her and go back to bed.

I thought I could hear her crying. She sounded scared.

Jonny it's not a kitten it's a fox. A fox cub. Now leave it alone and let me deal with it. All foxes are dangerous no matter how small.

Caroline didn't know why she had said that to Jonny. Of course it was an ordinary kitten, but she didn't have time to deal with his frantic nonsense.

Mrs Wilde? The operator asked.

Yes. Caroline was so tense she almost dropped the phone.

There is no problem on the line as far as I can tell. It seems as though she's left it off the hook deliberately, or perhaps knocked it off the table. That does sometimes happen.

Yes, thank you. Caroline replied. She hung up the phone. There were two telephones in Maria's house. Could they both have fallen off the hook? Caroline wondered. When she looked down she saw that Jonny had gone. It reminded her to look in on him and Ava. And the kitten, come to that. There was nothing she could do about Maria in this weather on her own.

Daniel was baking. He'd had a difficult day but he felt better now that he was sitting in the warmth of his kitchen making mince pies. He had a decanter of brandy next to him and he splashed a little into a pan with sugar and butter to make a sauce. He poured a splash into his cup of hot milk and swirled it together with a cinnamon stick. A cheeky treat that the girls didn't need to know about. He began melting dark chocolate in another pan, humming under his breath. He was getting ready for the little Christmas party he and the girls were going to have. Once the baking was done he had plans to put them all in their Christmas dresses and put on some records for dancing. He reached down to open the stove, when he heard a thud against the glass. Daniel raised his eyes but didn't get up any further.

Kids, he thought. Probably.

There was another thud and this was followed by laughter. But it wasn't a child's laughter. Daniel recognised the voice of the red faced man who had threatened him at the pageant. It was an ugly laugh that had no lightness in it. He said some of the words that Daniel was used to. He wondered why the stones didn't make more noise and why they didn't break the glass. He got up cautiously and peered through the crack in the curtain. The man aimed once more, from further away this time so Daniel could not hear his voice. He was only throwing snowballs. That was all. Just snowballs. And they were going away from Daniel's house.

Pervert! shouted Leo. He was in no mood.

Jed let him be. He didn't ask any questions and that was best. He'd been back to the car inside ten minutes. They had got back on track and now they were near the club. Too bad they ran out of juice near the pervert's house and had to walk the rest of the way. Too good to miss though, an opportunity like that. A bit of Christmas cheer.

PART TWO: THE MUSEUM OF ATHEISM

1900 1 OCTOBER

1900 1 OCTOBER

The Museum of Atheism was a bad place. Ava didn't want to go there. If you were dead you could go there, if you didn't love God. Her daddy had taken her there when she was a little girl to show her what would happen if she didn't love God, If she was a naughty girl and didn't go to church and sing and go to the pageants and show God how she loved him. Ava did love God, she loved him and she didn't want to go to the Museum of Atheism. She didn't even know how to spell it.

Ay-Thee-Iz-Um, her daddy had taught her to say it. And Jonny too but he was older and he was good at saying it already. Museum she knew, she had been to the museum in the city to see the dinosaurs. But there were no dinosaurs at the prison.

I'm going to take you both the prison today, Jed had said, Uncle Leo said its okay, the governor is on holiday and he has all the keys. Wouldn't you like to see what they unlock?

Ava had wanted to stay at home and paint the picture of the twelve dancing princesses she was making for her bedroom wall. She remembered how she'd been a bit of a baby, crying a little bit.

Come on Ava, it'll be awesome looking at all the rooms in the prison, please come with me. Jonny had said.

Uncle Leo's going to show us the Museum of Atheism. Her daddy had said. Ay-Thee-Iz-Um. He'd explained.

I know, Jonny had said.

Yes, but you don't know what it means.

Dinosaurs, Jonny had said.

You'll see, their daddy had replied and then said no more.

Ava remembered abandoning her painting and letting her mummy dress her for the cold.

The prison was scary. It was like a big grey house and there were sharp wires all around it. It had looked like the picture in Ava's book of the castle Sleeping Beauty got trapped in.

I don't like it, she'd said. I don't like the castle.

Her daddy had picked her up and thrown her over his shoulder and tickled her. She'd liked that but she still didn't want him to bring her inside.

Put me down Daddy, she'd said and he did, he'd let her walk but had put his hand in hers, his funny brown glove with fur on next to her blue mittens. She squeezed his hand and they followed Jonny who was running ahead to meet Leo with the keys.

Leo was standing in front of them. He had his prison outfit on. Ava had seen her mummy wash it in the basement. It was so ugly, grey and black. His boots had thin grey ribbons through them.

Why have you got ribbons on your boots Leo? They look funny. Ava had said.

Leo looked at her like she was stupid. He picked her up suddenly, without asking, and brought her face up to his. They're not ribbons sweetie, he'd said, and his mouth smelled funny to her, a horrible smell like when she cleaned her teeth with the nasty green liquid. They're leather thongs. He said. To keep my boots on in case I need to do any kicking. He laughed and Ava didn't know why that was funny. What do you feed her on Jed? Concrete? He said to her daddy. And she knew that concrete was what they'd used to make a place in the garden for the table and chairs. It was grey and stinky and no one would eat it. He put her down then and pretended she was too heavy to hold up. Ava was glad and put her hand back in her daddy's. Leo unlocked the front door and they went inside the castle.

The floor and walls were cold and Ava could see her breath. Jonny was excited and he walked just behind Leo, watching everything he did. They came to the end of a long corridor and there was a tall gate made of metal that Ava couldn't see to the top of. She looked behind her and couldn't see anything but more corridor. She gripped her daddy's hand as tight as she could and wondered whether something bad was going to happen.

Are we going to see the prisoners? Jonny asked. He did not normally talk to Leo at all and Ava was surprised.

No Jonny, we're not going to see the prisoners.

D'you reckon they're ready for it Leo, their daddy asked.

I think they've got to see it Jed. Leo replied.

See what? Jonny asked

Now I was talking to your daddy son, did I say, 'excuse me Jonny would you like to ask a question?'

I just wanted to know if . . .

Did I ask you Jonny? Did I say one word to you?

Ava was worried, why was Leo being so nasty to her brother?

Leo? She asked in her sweetest voice. He bent down.

Yes darling? He asked, his sticky breath blowing cold in the air between them.

Ava bit him on the nose as hard as she could and he screamed. The whole left side of his face went darker but there was no blood. He raised his hand but her daddy grabbed it fast.

She's a baby Leo; she doesn't know what she's doing.

Well Jed, don't ask me again if they're ready, ask yourself why you didn't bring them before. They're running wild. I brought Sue and Lori here as soon as they could talk.

Ava thought of Leo's children, they came over sometimes and pinched her and pulled her hair.

I think Sue and Lori are running wild Uncle Leo, she said, they have no manners at all.

Her daddy picked her up then and whispered to her to be quiet. She didn't mind, she felt happy. It was only the truth and she hated Leo for picking on Jonny. Jonny didn't look up at her. He was looking at the floor and didn't seem excited any more.

Here we are, said Leo as the big gate swung forward, the Museum of Atheism.

The first thing Ava noticed was the smell, it was like the zoo. She was frightened by it.

Is there a real dinosaur in here Daddy? She asked. He didn't reply but put her down on the floor. She looked for Jonny but she couldn't see him, the room was dark and there were lots of things in there.

Jonny, she called, but there was no reply. He must still be upset, thought Ava. Then she called out for her daddy. He didn't answer either.

She looked back to where she had come in and the door wasn't where she thought it was – the room looked different.

Leo? She asked, can you turn on the light? He didn't answer either. Ava was worried they'd gone to a different part of the room without her; she could see a light ahead of her and made her way carefully through the rows of shelves. She could see that there were scary things on the shelves, there were so many jars and each one had a single arm in it floating in yellowy water. She couldn't see them very well but they looked wrong. One had no fingers and another one had two hands coming from it. A few of the arms were as small as hers. She didn't want to scream because she could hear the noise of an animal nearby, she didn't want to show him where she was because it was a museum and museums had dinosaurs. She didn't even want to call out again because there was something wrong and what if the others had been eaten. Ava got down on all fours and crawled slowly along the shelves, peeking through so she could see but the animal could not hear her. It made a noise again, a kind of purring growl. Is that what a dinosaur sounded like? She wasn't sure. She crawled forward, and could see another row of jars, this time they were filled with eyeballs, but the eyes looked like they had been leaking, the colours in the middle mixed with the white part like when her mummy cracked a fried egg. There was another sound, a sound she understood. It was Jonny's snore, he always sounded the same when he snored, he made a little whistle. She crawled towards the sound and even though she was scared of the animal she couldn't help standing up and running towards it.

Jonny, Jonny wake up, said Ava as she ran. But when she finally made it into the light she stopped running, stopped shouting. For there lay Jonny cuddled up to a fox in a glass cage. The fox was rubbing its nose against Jonny like he was a baby.

And then Ava screamed because she knew the fox would eat Jonny and then eat her. She screamed for her daddy and he didn't come.

No one came.

PART THREE: REALFLESH

2000 24 DECEMBER – 0700

24 DECEMBER 2000

Chalice Lichen
Appearance: Upturned, chalice-like cup.
Effects: Superstitious belief that these mushrooms are used in satanic rituals.
Environment: Dead matter.

The curtains in Ava's room stirred as a draught filtered through the rotten window frames. The room was spattered with damp and creeping fungus. Jed had done half a job, buying white paint and covering the lumps. Leo was always saying how he'd do a few more jobs around the house but he didn't ever get round to them. The wall was covered in blood-black splotches that were wet to the touch. There was something beautiful about them, but Ava's breathing was shallow when she slept.

Ava was sleeping now. She breathed violently through her nose, drinking in the disturbed air. She moaned a little in her sleep and her little fists curled tight against her stomach. Her lungs rasped and finally she was forced upright by a spasm. She woke abruptly, coughing and retching.

The nightlight wasn't on. Ava reached out for it and there was a flash of blue light which hissed and went out. Ping, ping, ping. Ava pushed the nightlight on and off on and off but it didn't come on. She had been having a funny dream and it made her confused.

Mummy! She called, but not very loudly. She thought about the last time she'd had an accident. She didn't want to get in trouble again. She was getting used to the dark now, and the light from the moon was shining through her curtains. She stepped out of her bed and her bare feet felt nice on the thick carpet. There was cold air coming in from the window and Ava's wet legs dried off quickly, leaving her skin icy cold and her pyjamas sticking to her.

In the corner of the room where her lamp was plugged in, another bright blue light was crackling like a firework. It fizzed and went out. Her mummy had told her never to touch electricity so she stayed away. She thought it was better not to put the big light on in case that was dangerous too.

Ava took off her wet pyjamas and washed herself with a flannel and soap at her little washbasin. The curtains had blown wide open in the draught and Ava could see the snow had stopped falling. The moon was so bright she could see her face in the mirror, some of the black make-up had stained under her eyes and her eyes were stuck together with glue from her false lashes. She started coughing again, and felt too cold to stay at the sink, so she dried off and rolled her wet clothes in a bundle with her sheets. She thought she would sneak down to the basement and put them in the washing machine before anyone noticed. She shivered and needed to get dressed. Her mummy had laid out her Christmas outfit on the chair. Ava put on the clean vest and pants and the warm red tights. She stepped into the crisp, tartan dress and red cardigan. At last, she felt clean and warm. She grabbed the wet bundle and crept quietly out of her room.

The bulbs in the hall were flickering on and off, but Ava managed to make her way down the stairs.

Ava thought her mummy would be in the living room watching television, that's what she normally did at night. But the living room was dark too. There was no sound at all downstairs. Ava took her chance and sneaked towards the basement. When she was at the top of the stairs she reached for the switch. It didn't work. She turned herself around and crawled down slowly, backwards, one hand followed by one foot. The stone stairs were cold, even through her new tights, but she made it all the way down to the bottom. She squashed the bundle of clothes in the machine with some of her dad's undershorts and poured in lots of green liquid. Then she turned on the machine and walked back over to the foot of the stairs. She made her way back up the way she had come down, one foot, one hand, one foot. She got back to the top and felt the warmth of the carpet on her feet. She was still very cold, so she decided to go into the kitchen and warm herself. The orange light flickered through the door of the stove and she was drawn towards it.

Hello Sweetie. A strange, deep voice said, someone had been sitting in the dark and watching her. She didn't know who it was. She didn't want to go further into the kitchen but she didn't know where else to go. As she looked to her right, there was something on the table, something that looked like a lady in a silver sequinned dress. But her arm was twisted and she wasn't speaking. There was someone dressed in a big red cloak standing over the lady with a knife in their hand.

Santa? Ava asked?

There was no answer. The knife went through the arm completely and Ava ran. She ran into the downstairs bathroom and locked herself in. Last year, when Jonny had sneaked out to the treehouse, he had shown her how he did it. She thought she'd never do it because she was scared, but she was more scared now of Santa in the kitchen. She pulled the stool across to the window and climbed on it; she opened the rotten catch like Jonny had shown her, and jumped out into the snow.

Ava started to cough again. She gasped for the coolness of the air through her nasty breath. She didn't know where she was running. Her red tights were soaked through up to her knees now and she was sick of being wet and cold. She thought of her mummy and Jonny, she was worried that Santa would get them too. She needed to find someone to help her.

Daddy! Daddy! She shouted. She saw a man's back dressed in a sheepskin coat. Her daddy had the same coat and it smelled nice. He sometimes snuggled her up inside it and kept her warm, he even had a small, silver bottle in the inside pocket and he let her have a tiny sip of the drink inside. It felt like swallowing fire and it was magic. Like the steam from the tea or daddy's pineapple.

Daddy! She shouted again, but the man didn't turn round. She was worried then that maybe it wasn't her daddy. Maybe it was someone else. Maybe it was Santa.

Ava stopped shouting and started walking backwards, so she could get away from him but still see what he was doing. In the silence, she could hear her crisp footsteps and worried that the man would hear them too. But he still did not turn around.

Ava wanted to cough but she put her hand over her mouth to stop it. Then she heard another noise behind her, a howl. All she could think was fox, fox, fox. She stopped, not knowing which way to go. She curled herself into a tiny ball and shut her eyes tight. She couldn't help crying, she cried and cried and cried until she felt a hand over her mouth and felt two hands pick her up. The ground moved quickly in front of her as Ava and the person holding her ran across the valley. Ava closed her eyes and saw nothing. Her breathing slowed and she didn't see anything more.

A bitter flurry of wind disturbed the powdered snow and covered two sets of footprints. It was as though there had never been anyone there at all. The roads were covered in white drift and there was very little sound. There was a chill but it wasn't freezing. The landscape was muted by the snow and nothing but wind passed through. If anyone was out that night, you would barely be able to hear their footsteps as they dipped through the sifting white dust. Slow sounds fell through the air: feet making a path in the snow, wet, shallow breaths and tinny underwater noises of a cassette playing Christmas carols in someone's pocket. But nothing else. Nothing at all.

Consciousness came to the little girl slowly, like the dripping of candlewax. When she opened her eyes properly and looked up, she could see the cracks in the ceiling, cracks so large that the grey blanket of sky could be seen. No wonder she was shivering with cold. Her clothes and the mattress were soaking where the snow had melted into her. It fell still, not the powdery flurry of yesterday but big wet flakes. In a room like this there was bound to be fungus all over the walls.

The treehouse was a safe place, but it wasn't warm and it wasn't dry. The rope ladder had been replaced carefully, but it was treacherous all the same. Creeping damp had infected the wood and the floor felt soggy underfoot. In the corner of the room, where a stray firework had landed, was a dark, blasted hole.

Sweetie? Sweetie? Are you okay?

Ava threw her arms around the man. At last there was a smell she knew. Leather and wool and brandy. Her daddy's coat.

24 DECEMBER 2100

Flaky Gold Fleece
Appearance: Bioluminescent gold toadstool
Effects: Create light from organic matter
Environment: Fallen branches

Silver Bells, silver bells, it's Christmas time in the city. Ring a ding, hear them ring, soon it will be Christmas day.

The carols were on low in the club between dances. The girls were sitting at the bar with their customers. There was a lot of good champagne being cracked open and no one was counting the cost. No one except the girls whose job it was to ensure the tills were full and the men were extravagant. The club was sprinkled with blue and white fairy lights. The pole was sprayed with canned snow and the dancers had to keep reapplying it over the handprints they left.

It's so annoying having to wash that shit off your hands, Clara said to Ginny in the back. She had just come back from doing her dance and Ginny was getting ready to perform hers. They each had a theme tonight and Ginny's was arctic adventures. She was wearing a white fur-trimmed bikini with white body glitter. Her blonde hair was swirled on top of her head and completely covered in silver sequins.

I know, tell me about it, at least it matches my theme. You have to be careful not to get it on your fur.

I know, but I can just say that I'm a little bear who's been out in the snow I guess. I don't think anyone notices me until I've taken my bear suit off anyway!

Clara's theme was Wild Christmas. She had a cute little brown furry suit and ears. she'd set up an old carousel projector facing the blank wall and cast blurry images of forests and swamps behind her as she did her dances. As yet no one had come to congratulate her on her artistic choices.

Good luck. You look gorgeous Ginny. You need to be careful though, their hands are everywhere.

What's new? Asked Ginny and laughed as she walked out carefully on her high silver shoes. She turned back at the door, as Clara was taking a swig of cold beer.

Where are Jed and Leo by the way?

They were here a few minutes ago. I don't know. I didn't see them when I was dancing. Maybe they're talking to Bob.

Maybe, Ginny said. Maybe they are. She bit her lip and carried on out of the back room. As the door opened, Clara saw the flashing of a strobe light, set up to show off Ginny's icy glitter. The door swung shut and Clara was relieved. She'd had quite enough showbusiness for a while. She put her feet up on the dressing table and put on her reading glasses, pushing the bear ears higher up on her head. She opened her murder mystery novel and drank her beer in peace.

Caroline was a little cold and pulled her new Christmas dressing-gown tighter. She was drunk now. Earlier she'd been relaxed, then a bit merry. But now, she realized, she was stinking drunk. That didn't stop her pouring another glass of red wine. It looked pretty where the light from the stove gleamed through it, like liquid fire. It wasn't as though she were drinking whiskey, or vodka tonics. It was a perfectly respectable drink and it was Christmas and she had been working hard all day. She was still working hard now. She was fixing one of the dummies from Ava's dressing area. They never stayed in good condition because of the wear and tear they took. She'd been trying it out by dressing it in one of her pink peignoirs. The arm was still too loose, wrenched from its socket by one of the backstage people at one of Ava's recent shows. She couldn't think which. She thought she'd heard Ava a while ago, but when she'd looked there'd been no one there. She was getting paranoid, freaked out too easily. She felt embarrassed now about calling the operator.

Caroline took the filmy nightie off the doll and ran her fingers down the sides of the torso, where the seams would need to be stitched in with fine leather. That reminded her that she had to finish Leo's boots. He had to go in to work later, some sort of job for the governor. Apparently they got rowdy on Christmas night. He'd left them, gleaming, next to the stove and Caroline had to repair the leather thongs. He smelled, somehow of leather, like clean, cured meat. there was nothing tender about him, but when he ran his hands through her hair she'd felt that she wanted to do things for him, when he asked her to mend his boots she had no intention of refusing. He wasn't interested in her, only in her usefulness to him. They would be at the bar now, like they'd always been, like they'd been when she and Maria were dancers. They'd be running their hands over girls in silver sequined dresses whilst she ran hers over dummies in the drunken dark. She picked up her scissors and cut cleanly through the side of the doll to begin her repairs.

Six empty beer bottles sat in front of Jed and Leo when Ginny went to find them after her dance.

Hi guys, did you enjoy the show? She asked and sat on Leo's lap. Leo grunted, looked uncomfortable.

We've just been sitting here waiting for you to come over. We haven't got all night.

I thought you'd only just got here. Clara said . . .

Well Clara's not the brightest tool in the box is she?

The sharpest, Jed cut in.

Yeah she's got a sharp little figure if that's what you mean.

I mean, where were you? Ginny said.

How do you think these six beers got drunk if we weren't here?

Listen darling, you don't have to justify yourself to me, Lord knows it's none of my business. Ginny put her head on Leo's shoulder and looked up at him through false lashes.

Get off me. Leo said and pushed her away, but quite gently. All we want to know is whether you've sorted things out for later?

Ginny turned her back on Leo, her nostrils flaring but no change to her coy expression. When she spoke, it was to Jed.

It's all organised lovely. We'll shut up by midnight. Bob's going home at ten and then the show is ours.

Jed looked at Ginny tenderly and squeezed her arm.

You're a good girl Virginia, you never let me down. He slipped her a roll of notes and she palmed them. She walked to the back room as the music changed to a violin concerto and a spotlight appeared onstage. Mathilda was coming on covered in gold body paint and Ginny had a chance to take a breather. She winked at the dancing girl as she walked by the pole and flashed her teeth in a kind of gurning smile towards Bob, who was sitting in the corner looking miserable because his wife enforced a ten pm curfew on Christmas Eve. He didn't like handing over to Ginny, but it was cheaper than hiring anyone else. He didn't bother to smile back.

Jonny couldn't sleep. He was worried about the kitten. If it was really a fox cub then why were they giving her to Ava? He didn't know much about animals but he thought that foxes were a kind of dog, not cat. The kitten hadn't looked like a fox and she hadn't sounded like a fox either. He was used to their noise through his windows late at night. He stuffed his head under two pillows but the howls still got through. Once he'd looked out and seen the foxes together, one resting its paws on the other one and both of them

making a high wail. It reminded him of when Ava had been a baby if she woke in the night after a bad dream. He could hear the noise now and he pulled the pillows over his head. He knew there was no such thing as Santa, but he badly wanted to sleep all the same. Christmas was Christmas. He didn't want Leo to be there in the morning, he had his own stupid little girls to see, why did he have to live with them all the time? He didn't understand why his mum hadn't pushed him away, why his dad hadn't done anything. There was something going on and they thought he was too stupid to see. He wished he had stolen the key after all.

The howling continued and Jonny was sick of it. He took the pillows off his head and threw them off the bed. He kneeled up and looked out of the window. A draught was coming through because the frames were rotten and he shivered without the blanket. It had stopped snowing, and the mist had cleared, there was an almost full moon which meant that Jonny could see for a long way in the distance. He couldn't see any foxes even though they sounded nearby. He could something in shadow a long way away, near to the strange old man's house and almost at the strip club. He wasn't supposed to know it was a strip club. He wasn't supposed to know that his daddy went there but Ava had told him all about it. She'd been there and had her make-up done by the dancers. The exotic dancers. He was glad that he didn't have to talk about it to Leo because he thought he might call him a faggot for being scared to go and look. But the club looked fun and inviting. It was more Christmassy than their house. There was tinsel here, but it barely touched the empty space. Jonny would like to see so many pretty lights up close. It looked like a gingerbread house from the story Ava liked. He didn't like it, there was nothing scientific about a gingerbread house, it wasn't as exciting as Dismembered Man. But it looked warm, and fun. He could almost imagine he heard the music coming from there. But it must be his mum downstairs playing carols. Jonny felt better, whatever the foxes were doing it was far away. He picked up his pillows and snuggled back under the blanket, glad of the warmth.

Lou was performing her dance now. She was dressed to look like a naughty fairy. This was not the most spectacular thing Clara had ever seen, Lou always dressed as a naughty fairy. She looked more like a drunk fairy with mascara smudged around her eyes and a lack of balance. She'd had bad news on the phone. Her boyfriend wasn't coming up for Christmas after all. She didn't trust him when he said his dog was sick. He'd never mentioned a dog before.

Woo! Yeah! The idiots in the bar shouted, loving her act. There was something about an unfocussed, miserable girl swaying on stage that seemed to appeal to the audience more than Clara's woodland theme. Clara walked past her to where Bob was sitting with his sweaty, redfaced friends.

Listen Bob, Lou's had some bad news, she's upset. I'll do two extra dances but can't you let her go home.

What do you mean? You can do two extra dances anyway. I'd rather she did two extra because listen to this, they're happy, they're full of Christmas spirit, they're buying drinks. They'll all be buying her drinks too.

What's wrong with you? She's not fit. Clara felt herself about to cry. She hated how emotional he made her feel. He was a fucking pig. She wished she could afford to tell him.

Jed came over to them. She didn't know if that was going to make things better or worse.

Hey Bob, d'you mind if I borrow Cherry here? Thank God he'd remembered to use her stage name. I feel like buying her a drink.

Sure, sure, go right ahead. Bob smiled and patted Clara on the bum. She's all yours.

Clara took her chance.

D'you fancy buying Lou, I mean Lucky, a drink too? Two are better than one.

Sure I do, she's just finishing. What perfect timing.

Clara walked quickly to the stage and whispered fiercely in her friend's ear.

Listen to me, you're drunk and it's not safe. Now sit with me and Jed for a while, just until Bob goes. Then you can go home and I'll cover your dances.

Lou looked blankly at Clara; let her lead her over to the bar.

Champagne please. She said to no one in particular. Luckily for her Clara was there to prop her up as she slid backwards from her stool.

Jed returned from his conversation with Bob and ordered another bottle of champagne which was promptly stuck on someone else's tab. He poured drinks for the two girls, took another beer for himself.

Now listen Clara, and tell your friend, we can't afford for Bob to get suspicious, so any time you feel your principles getting in the way of our working relationship could you please let me know in advance so I can kill you and hide your body in the woods. He laughed so she could tell it was a joke, but at the same time he ran his hand over her thigh.

Where's Leo? Clara asked.

He'll be back, don't worry. Had to go to work for a while.

To the prison? At this time on Christmas Eve?

Sweetie, of all people you should know that the grind continues throughout the festive season. His hand moved further up and Clara stood up abruptly.

I have to go to the bathroom. Clara said, and left her friend leaning into Jed for support.

24 DECEMBER 2200

Plums and Custard

Appearance: Thin, webbed cap, yellow with fine purple veins.

Effects: Sweet, edible, plentiful.

Environment: Hardy fungus that can thrive almost anywhere.

What the fuck happened to you? Jed asked. His friend Big Chris had just come in and he had blood smeared on his forehead. He staggered into the bar and raised his hand, palm out, to the room. Even in the chaos of flashing lights it was evident that he had had a bite mark on the hand. There was fresh blood oozing through his fingers and darker clots at the centre. Some of the girls screamed and Big Chris grinned. He waved the hand in front of him and chased after Mathilda who squealed and leapt into Leo's lap.

Chris, this is important. I asked what happened to you? Jed did not smile, did not take the opportunity to join in the fun. He just stood up from his chair and faced Big Chris down. Lou teetered on her stool once her support disappeared and Clara ran in to steady her. She took the opportunity, now that Bob had left, to bring her to the back room so she could send her home in a taxi.

I'll be back with a cloth in a minute. Clara said to Big Chris. Why don't you sit down? She supported Lou and both girls got wolf whistles as they walked slowly and with difficulty through the bar.

Fox bit me. Big Chris told Jed, swaying on the bar stool Lou had just left, one of his bum cheeks slipping casually over the side. He pressed his palm flat on the bar and dragged it along, smearing the wood.

What the fuck are you doing? You know these girls have to clean up that shit. I hope you get splinters in there.

Ooh, I didn't know you cared. Which one are you fucking Jed?

Ginny's dance had started again and at that moment the strobe light came on. The whole room turned to look at the altercation. Big Chris sitting on a stool looked about as tall as Jed standing up, and Jed was not a small man. But Big Chris was drunk and wounded and he looked none too steady. He didn't even seem to realize that Jed was mad.

Jed raised his fist and as it cut through the air towards Big Chris's head it was dissected by the strong flashes of white light. Clara ran towards the men, bandages and a basin of water in her hand.

Jed, stop it you prick. She shouted.

It was too late, there was no way Jed could redirect that force. Clara dropped the basin of water and pushed Big Chris's head down on to the bar. Jed's fist did not connect and he fell forwards, on top of Chris.

I'll get a mop, Clara said. Bandage your own hand.

Well Jed, said Big Chris, I thought you was against the young ladies cleaning up after us. He laughed and reached for Jed's beer.

You better tell me what happened Chris. That does not look like a fox bite to me.

No? Well maybe it wasn't. Maybe you should talk to your friend Leo about what's going on down at the prison. Down at the Museum of Atheism.

This time Jed didn't wait for intervention. He knocked Chris out cold and left as the man toppled backwards from his stool.

Jonny had been thinking about Dismembered Man for some time now. It wasn't that he was a little kid with a storybook. He wasn't a baby. It was research. He knew that scientists did research before they made their experiments. He had a lot of notebooks with his ideas in, but he didn't want anyone to see them. Some of them weren't very good ideas but his latest ones were better. That's because he had Ava now to help him. All he had to do was ask her to lie on the metal table while he drew different parts of her body, or worked out the angles of her arms and legs, where the joints of her knees bent and if they were as flexible as her elbows. They were. A lot more flexible. So he had a lot of diagrams now of how a person worked. At least how a little girl worked. Dismembered Man didn't just used parts of people though; he was too smart for that. He sometimes sewed a knife on instead of a hand, or a hook. Jonny thought that was a bit tacky though, he wasn't interested in pirates. He sometimes used the eyes of a bird so he could see from far away and once he had taken the legs of a monkey so he could jump and climb. Jonny had wondered what would happen if Dismembered Man had the legs and eyes of a fox.

Jonny had all forty-nine issues of the Dismembered Man series under the quilt with him tonight. It was Christmas Eve and he couldn't sleep and he just wanted to. He also had his best notebook, the one with Ava's arms and legs in it. His torch was very bright and he could read easily under his covers. It did get a bit hot though. He decided to get some air.

The night was still clear and Jonny could see far in the distance. The lights of the strip bar were still on, but the lights in the old man's house were out. The ground was covered in powdered snow and it looked as though it was freezing hard. The spades were still stuck upright in the garden, throwing shadows in the moonlight. Jonny could see lots of tiny little lights moving around outside the strip club, they seemed to be coming nearer and moving into a kind of straight line.

The lights were a warm yellow, like his torch, and Jonny realized it must be a group of people carrying torches. Maybe their cars had broken down and they needed help. But it was strange, because there were so many of them. About ten in all.

Jonny was distracted by a yowling coming from outside. He knelt up higher and looked directly underneath his window. There was a beautiful fox, all white and covered in a dusting of snow. There was a dark streak at her mouth and she was crying. Jonny gasped, the kitten was all-white too. Perhaps she'd come to rescue her. Perhaps she knew what Jonny was thinking.

Clara was reapplying shadow round her eyes; she was giving herself little pockets of purplish-brown to look like a baby bear. She didn't care if there were brawls and leers and wall-to-wall bastards in the bar, it was Christmas Eve and she'd had a good idea. It wasn't her fault no one got it. Ginny had looked amazing in her body glitter, spinning through a metal hoop in the strobe light. But with all the fighting, no one had noticed anyway.

Ginny, you looked glorious as Crystal. We're wasted in this place.

I know sweetheart. I know. It's a bearpit out there. No good cheer whatsoever. Where's Lou now?

Lou's gone home; I put her in Pete's cab and asked him to look after her.

Didn't think he'd be working this late on Christmas Eve.

Are you serious? Think of the cash to be made tonight.

Speaking of that . . .

I'm still not sure Gin, I know you said you've done these parties loads of times and no one gets hurt, but I haven't. I feel bad enough stripping in front of these losers in here, I don't know how much more I can take.

What d'you mean? D'you think you're better than me? Ginny wasn't smiling when she spoke to Clara.

Come on Ginny, don't take it the wrong way. You know your way around people, they listen to you, I'm just this oddball girl in a bear suit with no idea what's going on.

Just kidding. Ginny said, flashing her professional smile. Let's open some more fizz. Everyone else is wasted, we may as well be.

Clara took a glass, because she didn't want to seem funny to Ginny, Ginny could take exception very easily.

Cheers. Ginny said. They clinked glasses.

I'm going to check on Mathilda, Clara said, she might want a glass. As she walked back into the bar she poured her wine into a plant pot. She had a quick glance round, saw that Big Chris was still slumped at the bar and Mathilda was occupied with a group of fat-headed red men. She winked over at Clara to let her know she could handle them. Clara was glad to get back to the comparative peace of the dressing room.

Top me up Ginny, she said, and swallowed her drink in one mouthful, before holding it out for more. I guess I'll do it. She said, Maybe I can buy an airfare to somewhere else.

That's the spirit, Ginny said, and gave her friend a hug.

Magdalena darling. You look magnificent in that dress. I'm going to make you a gold one like Ava Wilde had at the pageant. I don't have many pictures, but I can remember it almost exactly. You too Lucy, goes without saying. Daniel was sitting on the sofa in between the two girls, hugging them to death.

I know we've had better Christmases. Daniel stopped to take a sip of his hot whiskey, and you know, I was going to be good to that boy and his kitten. Even though you don't like new people, I was going to bring them in and introduce you, as it's Christmas. For all I know the reason he was here was to put fireworks through my door.

The girls were comforting to hold, their flesh was warm and supple and he could feel them hugging him back as he sank lower into the sofa.

What was that? Daniel sat up, put his glass down on the coffee table. He could hear a high keening outside. It sounded like a child crying, but then again it could be a fox. He immediately regretted sitting up so suddenly and frightening Lucy and Magdalena. They shrank away from him and leaned into the far corners of the sofa.

No, don't worry; I don't think there's anything wrong. It's definitely coming from outside, not inside, so don't get scared. Please don't get scared.

Daniel walked to the front door and looked through his spyhole. He couldn't see anything. He sighed and opened the front door, the sound got louder and louder and Daniel made his way out into the snow in his slippers, towards the desperate cry.

24 DECEMBER 2300

Wolf Slime Milk
Appearance: Sticky yellow spores
Effects: Cause instant paralysis leading to death.
Environment: Forest floor

Caro, Caro baby, where are you? Jed walked through his front door and saw that all the lights were off. She couldn't be in bed yet, it was early yet.

Caroline? Where are you? he lowered his voice this time, remembering that the kids were supposed to be asleep.

Jed? Caroline called back from the kitchen. I'm in here.

Jed locked the front door behind him and walked to the kitchen.

You've been drinking? He said to his wife. There was an empty wine bottle on the dresser and a half full one in front of her. On the table was one of the dummies from the basement. The arm was hanging off and a pair of scissors was sticking out of the torso.

That's a bit gruesome isn't it? Jed asked. It's Christmas, not Halloween.

What?

Nothing, I'm only joking with you. But what are you doing working so hard on Christmas Eve. We can have a little time to ourselves.

I've had plenty of time to myself. It's not much fun being

stuck in on Christmas Eve. Jonny going on about the kitten and having to fix this mannequin and no one here to talk to.

But you don't have to fix this mannequin, why are you doing it now anyway?

Well after I'd washed the potatoes and plucked another bird and put the presents under the tree there wasn't much left for me to do.

I thought you were going to spend some time with Jonny, tell him a few Christmas stories, look at the tree together? Jed put his hands on Caroline's shoulders and started to rub them gently, she didn't relax. Jed stopped, walked over to the radio and tuned it to a station playing old Christmas hits.

Silver Bells, silver bells . . . drifted out of the speakers and filled the dark room. This time Jed pulled Caroline's chair back and pulled her out of her seat. She was heavy and limp. He placed her head on his neck and his arms around her body. She weighed so little, had never gotten over her beauty queen regimen. He waltzed her slowly to the music, they were out of time but it didn't matter. Finally she leaned into him; let him lead her around the kitchen in the glow of the firelight. He kissed her neck and sang the words in her ear.

Soon it will be Christmas Day.

Listen Caroline, I know you don't like me getting too involved with the parties at the bar. But you know we can't turn down that kind of money. I mean, you used to do them yourself.

Yeah and then I got married to you and my life got so much better and I didn't need to do them anymore.

Come on, would you rather be hostessing and stripping like the whores down there?

They're not whores when they're looking after Ava though, are they, Aunty Ginny and Aunty Clara. They're all she talks about.

Come on sweetie, we have a very talented daughter. She gets a lot of attention.

Then an advert for snow clearance came on, the jingle

much louder than the record had been. Caroline looked up at Jed.

Where's Leo?

He's just down at the prison. He'll be home soon, but we've got a while.

What about Maria?

What about Maria?

He went there didn't he?

Yeah but only to bring the kids some little presents before tomorrow. And to give them a goodnight kiss. Maria had put them to bed so he didn't stay.

What about Billy?

I don't think he gave Billy a good night kiss.

But he's okay?

What's wrong with you Caroline? You don't believe me?

Of course I believe you. I don't know what's wrong with me tonight.

What was Jonny saying about the kitten?

Oh he was going on about feeding it or looking after it or something.

You didn't let him did you?

No I told him it was a fox and we should leave it alone. Caroline walked back to the table, poured another glass of wine and sat down.

You want one Jed?

You told him it was a fox? You're joking?

No. If you don't want one I'll have the rest.

Jed knocked the glass to the floor with the flat of his palm.

You told him it was a fucking fox?

Why not?

Why not? Do you understand what's going on here? You told Jonny it was a fox. Don't you think that might frighten him a bit? Don't you think he might start telling people that we have a fox in our attic?

Jed, what's wrong with you? Caroline stood up. I think you should clean that up; I'm going to check on the children, make sure they're not too scared. She walked out of the kitchen and towards the stairs.

Jed sighed and took a broom and began to clear up the mess he'd made.

Caroline walked upstairs; she saw Jonny still had his torch on in his room. She would go in and tell him to go to sleep in a minute. First she wanted to check Ava's room. The door was ajar, and there was a streak of blue light coming through into the hall from Ava's star lamp. She pushed the door and walked in. There was a chill in the air. The room was silent, except for the fluttering of the curtains. It didn't matter how many times Caroline tucked them in; they still got loose in the draught through the rotting window frames. She had asked Jed to replace them so many times now, and every winter it was the same, they had to wait for spring. You couldn't just go removing full windows in the snow. Ice had formed on the inside and there was a spattering of mould. Caroline rolled up one of the towels next to Ava's sink and stuffed it against the draught. She tucked the curtains in behind the radiator. It would do for now and the edge had been taken off the chill. She walked over to the bed.

Jonny had drifted off to sleep again. His comics were tucked underneath him and the torch was sticking out of the blanket, still on full power. He had his notebook clutched tight in his hand and was just turning over on his side when a scream woke him suddenly. His first thought was that the fox was in his room. He was terrified that the animal had come to get him. Terrified, he started screaming too.

Jed ran upstairs when he heard his wife and son crying out. He rushed into Ava's room and saw Caroline flinging clothes out of the wardrobe.

What is it? What's wrong? He asked, but he knew what she was going to say. The bedding was on the floor in a heap. Ava always slept curled in a ball with her hands making tiny fists. She buried herself under two quilts. He could imagine Caroline peeling back the first quilt, then the second, and seeing Ava gone. She had stopped screaming and was completely silent, and she was throwing everything in the room around, as though Ava might be hidden under a box of magazines or a pile of dolls.

I'll check Jonny, he said. Still Caroline said nothing. Jed walked across the landing to his son's room. Jonny had stopped screaming now. He realized that there was no fox in the room and he was being silly. He thought it must have been a dream.

Hi Dad, he said, pretending to be cheerful.

Are you okay? Jed said. I thought I heard you.

No, no. I just had a funny dream. I'm alright.

Ava didn't come in here earlier did she?

No, why would she come in here?

Yeah, I didn't think so; just checking she didn't see any of her presents.

But none of her presents are in here are they?

Or are they? Jed replied, tapping his nose on the side and laughing.

Cool. Jonny said. I can't believe you two are so good at keeping secrets.

Jed laughed back and tickled his son.

You shouldn't read so many of these horror stories before bed no wonder you have funny dreams. Jed scooped up the comics and piled them neatly on the floor, placing the torch on top.

Dad? Jonny asked, Were you out earlier? I saw a lot of lights outside near the, the . . . the treehouse. I wondered if you were looking for foxes.

No, I don't think anyone was doing that Jonny, there's a lot of Christmas lights about, maybe that's what you saw.

Maybe. Jonny said.

Go to sleep now, you don't want to be awake when Santa

comes down the chimney?

No.

Goodnight.

Goodnight.

Jonny snuggled under his blankets and closed his eyes as his dad left the room. Jed did not hear him creep out and sit against the crack in the door as Jed made his way back to Ava's room.

24 DECEMBER 0000

Peppermint Drop
Appearance: Glowing green spores which carry through the air.
Effects: Burn skin of plants and animals they come into contact with.
Environment: Tropical climates

By the time Leo got home it had started snowing again. Wet, heavy flakes that soaked though his trousers. His boots were filthy and he was tired. He checked his watch. Christmas Day. He said. I guess that's something to celebrate. He opened the back door and took off his boots. He was just starting to undo his trousers when he heard a cough.

Shit. He said. Jed and Caroline were sitting at the kitchen table, a bottle of whiskey between them.

Well Merry Christmas. Leo said you nearly got an early Christmas present Caroline. He laughed but no one else did.

Where have you been Leo? Caroline said.

What? You going to let her talk to me like this Jed? Jed said nothing.

Where have you been? She repeated.

I've been out earning a living so I can pay you for your rotten housekeeping. Leo said, but there was something about the way they were both looking at him that made him wish his flies were not undone. He reached for them, fumbled them shut.

What's the problem? He asked?

Ava's gone.

What do you mean she's gone? Have you checked everywhere? She's probably in the basement looking for her presents or something.

Thanks for that Leo, that's a very helpful observation, what you just said, that's been very helpful to me in looking for my daughter so thank you for that. What I want to know, for the third time of asking, is where the fuck were you this evening and what do you know about Ava?

What do I know about Ava? Leo whistled between his teeth. Aside from that she's a little whore? He was so mad now; he could not believe that Caroline would have the nerve.

Leo was about to leave the room, go up to get changed, he could hear that little prick Jonny whining upstairs, but he'd put his music on and block it out. He needed some time to think about what had just happened. But Jed blocked his way, shoved past him to the hall. He was even more surprised when Jed walked out to the hall and spoke very clearly, very loudly, asking for the police.

Merry Christmas Jed, Caroline, said Dt. Graeme Madden. He took off his cap and held it between thin, gloved hands.

Merry Christmas, said Jed. Caroline bent her head and said nothing.

Caroline sweetie, Gray just wished you a Merry Christmas.

I hear him, said Caroline. She did not raise her eyes.

Saw you out earlier Jed. Good hunting?

It was, it was. Shame you couldn't have been there.

I know it really is a crying shame.

Come through and have a drink Gray.

I won't say no, it is Christmas day after all.

Me and Caroline are on the whiskey now; she's had a shock so you'll have to forgive her being on the hard liquor. It's not her custom ordinarily, said Jed as he led the way to the kitchen.

Graeme laughed and shook his head at Caroline as she followed the men through.

Jonny's asleep, said Caroline when they reached the kitchen.

Graeme looked at her then.

Why don't you tell me what's happened here Caroline. Sit down and have your drink.

Caroline reached for a chair and sat down. She waited until Jed had poured a good amount of whiskey into her glass and she started talking.

Jonny was sitting at the top of the stairs. He hung back in case they could see him from the kitchen, but they all seemed too preoccupied. The light from Ava's star lamp was still streaming through the hallway and it half-lit Jonny's face. He had been waiting for them to go downstairs and talk since his dad had come in looking for Ava. He knew that his dad would never tell him what was going on so it was easier to hide and listen. He'd had to run and hide in Ava's room when Leo came upstairs, muttering to himself. Jonny had sat under her blankets, his body shaking and tears soaking into the wool. He hadn't wanted Leo to know he was crying. Jonny had heard Leo's heavy feet taking the second flight of stairs up to his room near the attic. He'd tried to calm himself down after that. Once he'd heard the doorbell go, he was so anxious to listen in, so he crept back out on the landing. He could hear Dt. Madden in with his parents. His mother's voice was clear and loud, but she sounded different to normal.

I went in to her room and shut the curtains. They'd blown open in the draught.

They'd blown open? What do you mean? Could someone have opened them?

Someone like who?

I don't know. Someone. Dt. Madden sounded like he was trying to be patient. Like Jonny's mum was annoying him. He was speaking slowly, as though telling a complicated joke.

Someone could have come in Caroline, Jed, and disturbed those curtains. If they did do that, if they were in Ava's room; that would be something we'd need to look into, right?

Right. Jed said.

Jonny was asleep.

Caroline, I know that, you told me that. We're not even discussing that now.

Jonny shivered from the top of the stairs. He didn't want them to come and look for him. He didn't want to hear any more about this. He crept slowly back into Ava's room and hid under the blankets. He curled up and let the corner of the quilt up to let the shaft of blue light shine right into his hands, a game he always played with Ava. Whoever trapped the light first would get their wish come true.

Jed, have you got anything to tell me? Asked Dt. Madden, and Jed, for some reason, found himself shaking. He picked up his glass and touched it to his lips. It was empty. He put it back on the table.

Jed?

I've been out this evening. I don't know. I just got home about a half hour ago and Caroline was doing some mending here at the table.

What the hell is that? Interrupted Dt. Madden, it looks good and dead whatever it is. He laughed.

It's a mannequin. Jed replied, his confidence restored by his friend's good humour. Looks like Caroline had her fun with it. He gave her shoulder a squeeze and laughed himself, a weak little bark.

And then, Caro went to check on Ava and she'd just disappeared. Just gone. So we called you.

Anyone else been here today?

Leo. Caroline said. Leo's been here, he's upstairs now. But he wasn't here and he wasn't with Jed. He said he was at the prison.

He said he was at the prison? Dt. Madden said, raising an eyebrow. Are you saying that you don't think he was there?

Caroline looked down at her hands. She didn't say anything. There were heavy steps on the stairs.

Jed looked to the door as Leo walked in. He looked like he'd had a wash and shave. Jed thought he'd like to have a shave himself. Some hot, soapy water might be just what he needed. His skin felt so dry. The cold wind cut through it and even though Caroline gave him lanolin soaks and sometime she put avocado on his face, it never felt clean. He thought of the skin he had when he was younger, the way his children looked when they were flushed from playing in the snow, the glittering skin of the dancers as they whirled round the pole. He sighed, stood up to get another glass for Leo.

Leo. Gray's come over to help us with this thing.

Yeah Leo, Caroline here said she didn't think you were down at the prison when you said you were.

Jed looked from Gray to Leo, he didn't look over to Caroline, but he could sense her slumping down further on to the table.

That right Caroline? said Leo.

Jed tensed, he thought it could be a bad situation developing right there at the kitchen table.

Well Gray, why don't you tell Caroline what you think about that.

Slowly, Dt. Madden walked over to Caroline's chair. He stood behind her. Leo and Jed stood by the stove, drinking fresh whiskeys.

Caroline, said Gray, I know you're upset, but you have to think about what you're saying. I know that Leo was at the prison, because he was doing a little job for the governor. It was a little job that I know all about, but we can't go telling everyone about it because it's confidential. So don't go worrying about where Leo was.

Caroline didn't say anything. She didn't even seem to move.

Now Caroline, I'm going to do all I can to find your daughter, she's a lovely little thing and I don't want her to come to harm any more than you, or Jed, or Leo do. Dt. Madden walked away from Caroline and over to the stove where the men were standing. Well, what shall we do? He asked them.

Jed looked to Leo and opened his mouth.

We need to go and find her. Leo said. Come on, what are we waiting for? There's beasts roaming and we're inside. Let's go and get the guns.

24 DECEMBER 0100

Devil's Tooth
Appearance: Sharp, ragged shoots.
Effects: Can cause blindness in mammals.
Environment: Deserts and dry scrubland.

Ava started to scream. There were two big dolls staring at her, their red lips slightly open as though they were going to eat her. Their eyelids flickered and they had sharp, long nails.

Sweetheart, what's wrong?

A man put his hand over her mouth and she was so surprised that she stopped screaming. He helped her to sit up and she looked around to see where she was. The dolls were bigger than her and there were lots of them sitting on the sofas. The man didn't look scary and he smelled comforting, like candy floss.

Who are you? Ava asked, still shaking.

I'm your Uncle Danny.

Uncle Danny?

Yes, I'm a friend of your father's. Now don't worry about getting in trouble for being so naughty and running away. Your dad is pretty mad but he asked me to look after you while he goes after the foxes.

The foxes? Ava asked and started to get scared again, I was running away from the foxes.

Yes and your daddy is looking after all that now. He'll come by in a while, or we'll take you back to your mummy. Don't worry; we'll have some fun here first. I'll just go and get some Christmas treats ready in the kitchen.

Ava was still confused. She didn't remember Uncle Danny but often there were new uncles. Her daddy worked with a lot of men. He seemed nice and he had a pretty room. She wasn't scared of the dolls now she sat up, they were just a bit big, that was all.

In the kitchen, Daniel's big hands dipped rhythmically under the soapy water as he washed his mother's tea set. It was duck egg blue bone china with gold rims. His spectacles steamed up but he didn't stop to wipe them. He didn't have time. There was never a spot of grease on Daniel's plates though. He liked the velvety feel of the hot water, the soap and grease rising to the top and the sharp squeak of a clean glass. He liked to rub the pads of his big thumbs around the crocks and along the knives and forks and spoons.

He muttered something to himself as he put them to drain and wiped his hands on his apron. It was just that he hadn't had a little girl to tea in some time. And this wasn't any normal girl, this was Ava Wilde! He needed to calm down. He couldn't just be acting like a naïve fan, wanting to take pictures of her and asking her about all her successes.

Mister? Ava shouted through from the living room. Can I have a glass of water? I don't feel too good.

Coming sweetheart. I'll bring you a glass of water in a minute. Call me Uncle Danny. He let the water swirl out and gave the tea set a wipe and polish. It was a good quality set and it had been invested in by his grandmother long before the era of dishwashers. He'd no sooner put his good china in the dishwasher than he'd put Ava in the freezer.

Daniel returned to the living room with a glass of lemon iced water on a tray. He leaned down to set it beside Ava and straightened back up, he had a shooting pain down his right leg, it would be best if he didn't do anything strenuous for a while.

Mister, are these your dolls?

What? Daniel was upset, he knew that certain crass people used that term, but to hear it come from the mouth of Ava Wilde, and in front of them! He was shocked and disappointed. He leaned down to whisper in her ear.

I don't want you to get frightened, but I need to take you outside for a minute. To have a quick word with you.

What? Ava asked, confused.

Daniel took her soft, peachy hand and led her out of the room. She was a little woozy on her feet but she let him lead her.

Ava darling, Daniel started.

How do you know my name? Ava asked suddenly, letting go of his hand.

Ava honey you're famous. You're a little star.

I'm a little star?

I have all your clippings. I'll show you when we've had tea.

I'm not hungry. I don't feel so good.

Listen Ava, I need to ask you something. Do you have any dolls at home?

Yes of course, Victoria Plum and Fairy Ellen.

Well do you love them very much?

Yes, Ava said rubbing her face with both hands. She looked very tired.

Well would it hurt their feelings if someone came into your room and met Victoria Plum and Fairy Ellen and said that they weren't real, that they were just dolls?

Jonny says it but I don't listen, I put my fingers in my ears.

Well in there, those girls are the same to me, it hurts me and it hurts them to call them dolls. Really, they're my friends. Especially Lucy and Magdalena. The others are here for business reasons.

Business reasons? Like money? Ava asked.

Like money, yes.

How?

I fix them if they get hurt, Daniel winced thinking again of the messes, the tears.

Can you fix my dolls? Ava asked, suddenly interested.

What's wrong with them?

They all got tammgled up.

Tammgled up?

Daniel blinked twice in the gloomy hallway.

Do you mean tangled? They're stuck together?

Yes, Jonny stuck three of the baby ones together. I can't take them apart. Mummy said I needed to bring them to the doll hospital. But you have a doll hospital don't you?

Daniel felt scared when she mentioned her mother. He didn't want to worry about all that now. He imagined pretty little Ava with her blond ringlets rolling a pink plastic baby carriage back and forth with doll's limbs sticking out at all angles.

Well, can you fix them?

Her teeth were missing, she had maybe two small ones lurking in the dark hole of her mouth and the words came out funny, a bit slurred.

Sure I can fix your dolls honey. I have a dolls' hospital outside.

Mrs. Nowakowski told my Mummy that there was a new dolls' hospital. She told her at church.

The long name came out in a soft foamy spray from the girl's toothless mouth.

Did she now?

Yes, she's friends with Mummy and she's married to Leo who lives with us.

Well she's right of course. Why don't you come along one day after Christmas and I'll see if I can fix them?

Daniel imagined the knot of rubber legs in the pink carriage.

Do you want to see my workshop? He said on a whim. I could show you how I fix the girls.

The girls?

The dolls he whispered, looking over his shoulder to the living room as he spoke.

The dolls' hospital? Ava asked.

The dolls' hospital, he said.

Daniel put one of his big coats around Ava's shoulders and wore one himself. He opened the back door.

Sometimes there're strange words on there, but don't worry about it, it's just silly people making a fuss.

Ava was standing at eye height to then dribbling red 'v' in 'pervert', and in his distraction, Daniel fumbled the wrong key into the lock at first; only getting in after a couple of attempts.

Ava's eyes widened as she took in Daniel's room. Every surface was covered in paintings of little girls. They looked as though they had been copied from greetings cards or children's book illustrations with their wide eyes and big bonnets. Some had horns or rabbit ears or tiny flaccid penises. Some were painted on to greaseproof paper and shone like little ghosts where they had been stuck to the windows. Notebooks covered most of the floor, stacks and stacks of typewritten entries that were covered with drawings of flowers and anatomically perfect vaginas. The shelves held gold crosses, statues of the Virgin Mary and tall white candles. Glow-in-the-dark rosary beads were strung between them like paper chains at a birthday party.

Wow Uncle Danny, you've got so much pretty stuff.

Ava wandered over to the workbench and saw the two dolls he was working on; one had an empty eye socket and the other was missing an arm. Both had blond ringlets and red velvet dresses. They looked a lot like the little girls in the picture.

Did they get tammgled up too?

His heart ran cold, the way she mispronounced her words, it was too much. Uncle Danny, what's wrong? Why are you making that noise? Are you sad?

Nothing Ava, nothing. I'm fine.

I'm cold now.

Me too. Let's go back inside. We can have tea now.

Uncle Danny? Ava asked when they were back in the living room.

Yes sweetheart?

I think you should call my Mummy now, I think she'll wonder where I am.

Well we can do that in a minute. You know it's rude to come to someone's house and not take tea with them.

But I didn't come here. I don't even remember how I got here. I remember I was scared of Santa coming to get me, but I don't know why. He's a nice man; he wouldn't come to get me. I just got confused. And then I ran outside and I thought the foxes were coming and then I don't know what happened. I just remember waking up here.

I told you what happened sweetheart. Your Daddy was out hunting the foxes and he asked me to take care of you for a while. I'll take you back to your house soon and you can go back to bed.

Daniel looked anxiously out of the window. He had a set of binoculars but it would look strange to Ava if he used them. If he could just work out that they were definitely out hunting, he could run over with Ava and tell her to crawl back in through the side window. They'd never need to know anything had happened. But if she didn't, if she made a fuss or a noise, there'd be trouble. And what if she said she'd been at his house. He was an idiot to show her the workroom; she'd be able to identify it easily. He could just tell the truth but it didn't sound too good either. Especially after what had happened earlier with the little boy. He was an idiot to care about people. If he could just ignore them all he'd never get into any trouble. But even then people were putting fireworks through his letterbox and graffitiing his walls.

Uncle Danny? Ava asked. Are you okay?

What?

You were talking to yourself about nasty boys. My brother is a nasty boy sometimes. I just pinch him if he upsets me.

Thank you Ava, I'll remember that.

It's okay Uncle Danny, Ava said, seriously. But my head hurts. Have you got some ice?

I'll go and boil the kettle and I'll bring in tea and ice and then we can look at your clippings.

Okay. I'm going to lie on rug now.

Ava closed her eyes and curled up on the rug in front of the fire, her tiny fists closed.

Daniel boiled the kettle in the kitchen. He put jasmine tea in the pot and poured the water on. On a tray he placed slices of lemon and mint, seven cups and saucers, seven plates and a stollen cake with a knife. It was heavy and he knew he needed to be careful so he placed the tray on a hostess trolley. He took an ice pack from the fridge and put it beside the tray. He wheeled it into the living room. He was just about to pour for everyone when the telephone rang.

Ava sat upright, confused. What's that? She asked. Is my Mummy here to collect me?

No darling. Said Daniel, we'll just let it ring. No civilized person would call at this time of night.

But what if it's my mummy? Ava started to whine.

The noise of the telephone didn't stop. There was no answering service on the line, Daniel didn't like them.

What if it is your mummy, he thought, *what if they've already noticed you've gone?*

I'll just go and check, he said with a big smile. He walked to the hall and pushed the door of the living room shut. He picked up the receiver and spoke into it very quietly, behind his hand.

Hello?

This Daniel Cooper?

Who's speaking?

Dt. Graeme Madden.

Detective . . . ?

I believe I asked you a question.

Yes this is Daniel Cooper. What's wrong?

Well I'm just making a few calls, just wondered if you'd seen anything out of the ordinary tonight?

Out of the ordinary? Do you mean the foxes?

No, not the foxes, I just mean anything out of the ordinary. No, no.

What about the young boy who fell into your garden?

Kids are always playing in that treehouse, it's not safe.

No, I shouldn't have thought it was. Boy was wearing a coat of yours, don't you want it back.

Yes, of course. I'll collect it next week.

Daniel could hear Ava singing in the next room, he was worried that she could be heard down the line.

If that's all?

Do you think I called you at one in the morning on Christmas Eve because I care about your coat?

No.

No?

I'm sorry, what were you saying?

Are you nervous Daniel? You seem nervous.

I'm fine. Just a little tired.

You haven't seen Ava Wilde then, at all, this evening.

I saw her at the pageant this afternoon.

You like going to the pageants do you?

I'm a dressmaker. It's for research.

Dt. Madden didn't seem able to contain his mirth at that.

Uncle Danny? Ava called out, Is that Mummy?

Sorry I can't help you. Daniel said firmly and slammed down the phone. He walked back to the living room.

Yes sweetie. That was your mummy. She said I should just drop you back home. She's not angry.

Ava perked up. Yay! I was a stupid baby, but I want to go back now. Thanks for the cake and showing me all your pretty things. I'll bring the dolls next week. I'll ask Mummy to bring me.

Yes sweetie. Daniel said distractedly. He put his big coat back on and wrapped Ava in several layers. He put a hat and gloves on her and two pairs of thick socks. She looked like the prize in pass the parcel. Now, we're going to get into my truck, so I'll just go out and warm the engine up. You wait here in the warm.

Daniel walked out on to his drive, there, lying in front of the porch was the bundle of bones, as though someone had put them there. Daniel was in too much of a hurry to do anything but step over them. He was really up against it this time.

24 DECEMBER 0200

Ghost Fungus
Appearance: Translucent white fronds
Effects: Hallucinogenic
Environment: Dark, wet places.

Jonny was comfortable in Ava's room. He could smell her on the blanket and two of her hairs glinted in the light of the star lamp. He knew he couldn't ask what had happened to her, but he was scared that he might know. Jonny curled up in a tight little ball, like he had seen her do so many times. He let the blankets close over him until he couldn't see the moon, or the blue light, and couldn't hear the sound of his mother crying in the kitchen. He drifted off to sleep, exhausted, but he moaned and sighed as the wail of the foxes drifted through the cracks in the window.

What exactly are we hunting here Leo?

Big Chris was still swaying, propped his hat higher on his head with the business end of his rifle as he asked.

Be quiet Chris. You know we're not hunting anything. We're going to get that little girl back from the pervert. Leo replied.

Yeah, if he's got her Leo. Jed said. There was a sudden silence when he spoke, as though the men remembered why they were there, that it wasn't just some kind of hunting trip, but a man's daughter was at risk.

Yeah Jed, but we know he has her, he tried to take Jonny earlier and he's a fucking pervert. Leo was belligerent, still sipping from his silver flask. He offered it round but there were two cracked sores on his mouth, everyone could see them, even in torchlight.

The men wore their heavy winter clothes, with coats done right up to scarfed faces. Every one of them had something round their mouths and noses; a bit of cloth, a handkerchief, cleaning rags.

Lou instinctively reached up to her own bare mouth. She wished she had something too, to cover the sound of her breathing. Bob hadn't told her what to look out for, just told her to follow the group of men. But now she was in the thick of the group, and if she slipped, or stepped on a dry branch, she was done for. The wind had dropped and the night was now clear enough for them to see her if they turned around. She had never followed anyone before, and all she could do was hide behind one tree, wait for them to move on, and hide behind another. If it came to it she could pretend she was still too drunk and didn't know what she was doing.

One of the men let out an unpleasant laugh and the sound startled her. Luckily no-one could see her hidden behind the big tree and she collected herself at once. When the last of the men was nearly out of sight she crept out and started to follow them, keeping well back.

Filthy buggers, she heard Big Chris say. And then, there was almost complete silence. They didn't say anything else to each other but all seemed intent on keeping perfectly quiet. Their steps became more measured as they walked across the valley, tiny little pin-pricks that didn't shift anything underfoot. Leo had had a torch but he turned it down, so there was only a thin white streak. They all followed it like it was a rope and they were climbing a mountain.

We don't want to give him any ideas. Leo had said.

She was too close now, she should hang back again, but what if she lost them?

There's something there, behind the tree. Leo shouted, forgetting his own rules. He took his rifle and aimed.

Don't shoot Leo, we don't know what it is, it could be . . .

The sound of the gun firing cut off Jed's words, he had been about to say the name of his daughter. There was a scream. And it didn't sound anything like a fox.

Lou thought of burnt rice. Of the smell of it sticking to the pan in dark, brittle clumps. It was like the absence of sweetness. So dry, so dark and dry. She put her hand up to cover her mouth and nose, to protect them from the smell. She couldn't lift her arm; it twitched at her side but wouldn't do any more. The sound, the terrible sound and the smell. She didn't look, didn't have to, to know what they meant. Vomiting, she curled over and thought of nothing. Retching and retching and with it a screeing howl she tried to make sense of why she had been shot. A violent beating of wings began as a rook awoken by the disturbance took angry flight. Leaves scattered over Lou as soft and deep as snow.

Jed stared after the screaming bird and ran over to the bleeding girl. It wasn't Ava. Steam rose from the hot wound, like from the inside of his father's pigs when he had slit them as a child, making careful incisions in the bladder and stretching it like linen into squares to wrap the entrails in. He could wrap this girl's heart in fresh snow like a party favour and save it, he thought, and then he fell face down in the snow, shaking.

Caroline poured herself one more whiskey. She put plenty of soda in and six ice cubes. She didn't care for too much drink and she didn't find it was easing her anxiety at all. Still, she wasn't going to sit there in the cold, alone, waiting for news of her daughter, and not take a drink. She never knew what the men were up to these days.

Caroline opened the curtains in the kitchen and looked out over the valley. She used to love being able to see the open space in front of her. To look across and see the few small houses dotted around, the church in the distance, the town hall. Since the foxes had become wild, she cared less for the view. Though she could rarely see them, she didn't like to consider the possibility that they were out there. Tonight, it was chaotic. There were the lights of the torches carried by her husband and the men with him, men who were helping to find her daughter. But Caroline knew already that her daughter would not be found.

The snow had frozen over in hard layers, and there was still more falling. If Ava was out in that, without shoes on, she wouldn't stand a chance. She should have told Jed to bring boots with him, her little wellingtons with the pictures of star fish and spiders that Jonny had drawn on with magic marker as a birthday present. But then she would have had to tell him that she knew Ava had no shoes on when she left. And that would lead to all sorts of trouble.

Caroline could not talk to Jed any more. She couldn't ask him for help and understanding; she couldn't explain the fears that gripped her recently. She thought about calling Maria Nowokowski. She thought about calling the girls at the strip club. Jed and Leo spent so much time there, they said on business, but she knew what kind of business. And it gave her no comfort to realize that they had little but contempt for the girls working there. She had been one of them after all. The first time they'd come in, fifteen years ago, they'd been a regular double act. Both were handsome, Leo in a brutish way and Jed with his charm. But Caroline had seen where her best chance lay.

She'd let both of them take her out, but she'd gotten serious with Jed. He'd been so romantic then. Taken her away to Hawaii. They'd been out in a boat one day. Jed rowing.

Caroline had never been on the water before. The colours she'd imagined, the sparkling foamy layers that had seemed so exciting in the distance had thickened into a melting pool of grey. She had tested the coldness with one hand, trailed it in. The water had been freezing and rough. She had thought of how ferocious it would be down at the bottom where those layers ended and the seafloor began. Infinite cruelties, waiting teeth.

Here, Jed had said softly to her, as though not to startle her.

The first trip out on the sea can out people in a funny mood, he'd said. Anything out of the ordinary can cause upset.

He'd given her a rough blanket which had felt warm and dry; he'd kept it under his legs. She had taken it from him and then snatched back her hand, hoping he'd not seen how it shook.

Can be rough sometimes. He'd said.

Caroline had nodded, her painted lips twitching up, a kind of smile. Remembering herself. But she hadn't moved any closer.

When will we get there? She remembered asking, looking at the grey water. There was nothing in the distance. The late sun had made a haze of the horizon. He'd been taking her to see where he had grown up, a little paradise island. It was so far from the snowy valley where Caroline had been born.

He'd looked amused and said in a maddening voice.

Oh not too long. It always comes up sudden on you. Just hidden behind the rocks. You'll know when we get there alright.

With that cryptic answer he tipped the ugly brown hat over his eyes and sprawled back in the warmth. Caroline had thought he might be sleeping. She'd panicked, thinking what could she do if the boat needed steering or if there was a storm. Maybe it wouldn't be so bad to be drowned here. Maybe.

Her thoughts had trailed off and she leaned in a little

closer to him, looking at the length of him, the size of his arms. She remembered looking too at the red bristle on his top lip, remembering the fuzzy taste of it in her mouth. She'd had two yellow thumbprints on the inside of her arm where he had pressed her to him. She could recall the feeling when she'd run the tip of her finger along them, feeling the thrill of pain and imagining the swirl of his thumbprint melting into hers. She always felt inert with him, consumed. She'd mistaken his violence for passion and her passion for love. In the boat, in the middle of the water, her mouth had gone completely dry.

There had been a sudden rush of water behind the boat, throwing it off course and nudging Caroline forward right on to his lap. She'd gasped, closed her eyes, and felt the spray on her face. She'd bent to kiss him thinking it would be alright it would be alright after all. She'd tasted the dry furze of his beard where the salt had collected and she'd kissed him with her dry mouth. His lips had been closed and she'd felt his hands digging into her flesh.

With one careful move he'd pushed her back to the other side of the boat without even opening his eyes.

Caroline remembered sitting under the blanket, fuming. He had humiliated her. Hot shivers had gone through her hands and feet. The cool spray had died down and the sea became calm again. Jed had sat up, pointed them back in the right direction, and taken out the oars, rowing violently to land. She'd looked at him, blithely scanning the horizon, and willing him to look back, to see the contempt she had for him.

Caroline, he'd said at last. Caroline. Again.

She'd turned her head very slowly, shielding her eyes with a hand against the midday sun. For an instant a cloud flashed grey and she saw the shape of his mouth clearly as he muttered a word under his breath. The word 'whore'.

What? She'd said, unable to comprehend.

You think I don't know about you and Jed? He'd said.

They had been in the middle of the ocean. There was no

one around. She'd thought very quickly, very quickly.

I'm pregnant. She'd said. With your baby.

How do I know it's my baby? He'd asked.

How do you know it's not? She'd replied.

By the time they arrived at the island, they'd patched things up.

24 DECEMBER 0300

Mermaid's Weeds

Appearance: Slimy dark green fronds. Each frond oozes a healing green liquid when cut diagonally.

Effects: Universal antidote: reverses effects of all fatal fungi.

Environment: Near deadly fungi.

Slowly, Jonny began to wake. It was completely dark and he could not understand where he was. The starlight had flickered and gone out, the battery flat. It had been the noise which woke Jonny; the sound of a gun being fired, a woman's wails, and the siren of the ambulance as it drove straight over the frozen pond. As he sat up and threw off the quilts, bright lights cut through the thin material of the curtains, turning the room electric blue. Nothing was where it was supposed to be, the sheets were all tangled up around his neck and he felt freezing cold. Water, he needed to drink some water to get the taste out of his mouth. Jonny's tongue felt thick and dry and he could not move it around inside his mouth. He couldn't understand why the sink wasn't in the same place as usual; his superman beaker wasn't beside the bed. He felt sick, with a stomach pain. As the blue lights stopped flashing and a clearer, white light filtered through the curtains, the room became less blurry and Jonny realized the problem. He wasn't in his own bed, but in Ava's room. For the minute he couldn't understand why he was there. Where was Ava? One thing he did remember was the kitten. He had to go and check that she was alright.

Jonny got out of bed and shivered. He walked to the bedroom door and removed Ava's dressing gown. It was white, with little bear ears. He pulled the hood up as well, he was so cold. Jonny walked across the hallway in his bare feet, stopping at the door to his parents' room. The door was half open and he pushed it all the way. He turned on the light. Jonny took the chair from his mum's dressing table and placed it on top of the made bed. Without fear, he climbed on to the wobbling structure and took the key from the hook. He stepped back on to the bed, then the floor. Putting the key in the pocket of Ava's dressing gown, he replaced the chair.

Jonny turned the light off and walked back across the hall, then upstairs to the second floor. He didn't go up there often because that was where Leo's bedroom was. He had heard so many strange noises coming from up there recently; he didn't think it could just be the kitten though. She was so small and she just made a little squeaking sound. He was so worried that she would be scared or lonely. That she would be locked up all alone without him. He started to cry. He was shaking and tears leaked down his face. He thought of how he had abandoned the kitten, how his parents had left her locked up in the attic, and he couldn't stop crying. He wiped his tears with his sleeve and unlocked the door with the key. It was a very heavy door, and he had to give it a good swing. He could hear the kitten mewing loudly and he knelt down to pick her up. She jumped into his arms and he buried her inside the white dressing gown. He could feel how warm she was, wriggling next to his heart.

There was another sound, louder than the mewing; it was almost like a growl. Jonny wondered how the kitten could be making such a loud noise. He looked up and saw two pairs of amber eyes glinting in the darkness. The growling was getting louder and he could feel the creatures pacing. Jonny stood up and began to back out of the attic with the kitten. That was when the first fox pounced. Jonny screamed, feeling teeth close round his ankle.

Caroline did not shout to Jonny as she made her way quickly upstairs. She knew, without a doubt, what she had to do, the kitchen knife in her right hand. It had been long months that they'd kept the foxes up in the attic. Usually she sedated them with their food but it had been such a long day today, and she had been so upset about Ava, she had completely forgotten. What she couldn't understand was how they'd broken through the door. Jed had reinforced it with steel; he didn't want to take any chances. Caroline took two steps at a time, in spite of her fuzziness. The scent of fox must and her own sharp sweat cleared her head. She reached the top floor, heard Jonny's screams get louder. It was the vixen who had him. She was grazing his leg with her teeth, playing with him. It would only take a second for her to bite clean through to the bone. Caroline did not offer her son any words of comfort, there was no time. Instead she took the kitchen knife and plunged it through the vixen's oesophagus, severing her carotid artery. Her jaw spasmed and Jonny's leg was freed.

Get back Jonny, if you can walk, get down the stairs now. Caroline was tearful.

Jonny's leg was only hurt superficially, he stood up and ran, the yelping cub still tucked in his dressing gown. Caroline pushed the door shut on the dying vixen and her mate. She followed her son downstairs, the knife still clenched in her shaking hand.

What's going on? asked Clara. She and Ginny were sitting in the empty club, waiting for the men to arrive. I can't stay here all night until they decide to come.

The thing is that they have to say they're going out hunting foxes, they can't say they're out hunting foxes unless they really are hunting foxes. You can see right across the valley from most of the houses.

I think I'm going to go home; it's been a long day. I've drunk so much I've gone back to sober, but with a headache.

Let's go and look out the front, maybe we can see something. I don't want to let that kind of money go now that I've waited this long. Ginny replied.

The two women walked to the front of the club and pulled back the black shades.

Oh shit! Said Ginny, there's blue lights everywhere.

Do you think Bob found out about the party and told the police?

Oh shit, I don't know.

Fuck this. Come on. Get your coat, let's get out of here.

Ginny and Clara pulled the drapes shut and turned off all the lights, they walked to the back room and did not bother to take off their outfits or makeup, they simply pulled on sweaters and coats and scarves. They unplugged everything, turned off the lights, locked the takings in the safe and let themselves out the back way.

They had to walk across the valley, near the lake, to get home. As long as there was nothing going on at the club they couldn't be held accountable for any problems. The lake was almost completely solid now. There was a tiny unfrozen corner near the waterfall and they could see three or four ducks floating there, pecking at the ice.

I wish we had some bread, said Clara, they make me feel sad.

Ginny skated on her boots across the frozen lake and felt the exhilarating rush of icy wind across her face. She came to a sudden stop next to an ambulance parked on the other side.

Clara! She called, there's been an accident.

Clara skidded across the lake to meet Ginny. By the time she arrived they could see Lou screaming and thrashing her arms and legs with a trying to calm her down.

Where does it hurt Miss?

Lou screamed again.

Carl, he called to the second medic, we need to get her on a stretcher and into the ambulance.

Lou looked up at him, her eyes glassy and cold. She stopped thrashing and seemed to understand that he was there to help her. He walked over to the back of the ambulance, and he and the second man lifted the stretcher between them. They placed it on the snowy ground next to Lou and prepared to lift her on to it.

This got called in a few minutes ago, male, didn't leave his name. I don't understand why there's no one else here, said the paramedic as he snapped on latex gloves.

Maybe he had to go and call from a house, you know what phone reception's like at the best of times, and these are certainly not the best of times.

Lou whimpered, she couldn't speak, didn't want to speak.

The two men crouched down beside her and rolled her body gently on to the stretcher with practiced hands. Steam rose from the snow where drops of hot blood fell, and the two men got her into the ambulance with speed. She closed her eyes and let the pain wash through her, there was no way she could fight it.

Then she was in the back of the ambulance, an oxygen mask over her face, clean white cloths pressed to her arm and the man with the beard was sitting next to her, holding her hand in his gloved one. She felt better; they'd given her something to help the pain.

The ambulance drove off and the blue lights and sirens came on. Lou thought it was absurd that all this fuss should be for her. The man with the beard spoke softly to her.

Now I'm going to take the mask off for one moment, please don't be alarmed. Just so that you can tell me if there is someone we should call. Okay? He squeezed her hand and she felt safe, calm, almost blissfully relieved.

Bob, Lou said as the mask was removed. Bob sent me; he

knows what's going on.

Bob? Bob who?

Bob from the club. Lou said, her words getting heavier and more difficult. She couldn't think of names, numbers now. It didn't matter, nothing really seemed to matter and she couldn't imagine why she'd been crying like that before.

The paramedic replaced the oxygen mask and she closed her eyes.

You're not going to believe this; she just said that Bob Parker from the strip bar is mixed up in all this. You better call this in to the police station; we're going to need an officer standing by at the hospital. We'd better keep an eye on her.

Can we come too? A tall girl covered in silver glitter asked the medic.

Yes, please, can we?

We don't ordinarily allow more than one person in the back of the ambulance. Are you her friends?

Sisters, the little one said, she was wearing bear ears and looked like she had a black eye.

Let them. Carl said.

Is your daddy Bob up at the club? He asked, laughing. Better to keep them all together until the police came. He was going to call Gray Madden directly.

24 DECEMBER 0400

Kidney Lichen
Appearance: Kidney-shaped brown clusters.
Effects: Cause an unquenchable thirst.
Environment: Mountains.

Two frayed twists of rope swayed in the wind. They were all that remained of the severed rope ladder to the treehouse in Daniel's yard. It now lay coiled on the floor of the treehouse, next to Ava. There were marks around her neck where the rope had been pulled taut. Not clean circles but livid blurs all the way down to her icy collarbones. Ava's bare feet were bluish white, and droplets of ice began to form in her blond ringlets, along her pale eyelashes. Next to her body was a scrap of bloody silver material, a pile of tiny bleached bones and a square of matted fur. A small bowl, still steaming, lay beside her head. Four large toadstools were simmering in the broth, which smelled of burned sweetness, like rice pudding, like a gunshot wound.

A gloved hand closed her eyes, but the fear was still visible on her face. She had been quiet enough, in the end. A professional, a real lady.

I want to take the kitten, I want to take the kitten, I want it! Jonny shouted at his mother as she tried to take the fox cub out of his arms.

Okay Jonny, I don't have time for this. If you want to keep it, keep it. I have too much to do before we leave.

Jonny sat on the kitchen floor, still wrapped in Ava's white gown and with a bandage on his ankle. He cuddled the cub and rocked gently back and forth as Caroline dragged a chair to the tall cupboard next to the refrigerator. She stood on the chair and reached for a cake tin. There were notes in it; she put them in her jeans' pocket. Leo didn't think she saw where he stashed the money, but he'd need to be a lot less drunk than he was to manage that kind of discretion.

Mummy? Jonny asked and Caroline didn't look at him.

Mummy? Where's Ava gone? I couldn't see her in the bedroom.

We've got to go now Jonny, I'll be back in a minute. I just have to pack a few things.

Caroline leaned down and kissed Jonny on the top of his head. He smelled of Ava's cherry soap. Caroline stood up straight, and walked out of the kitchen, towards the stairs.

Where's Leo? asked Big Chris.

I think he shot something back there, think he went to pick it up.

No, Jed shot something. Jed went to pick it up.

Who's asking about me? Shouted Leo, he was red faced and sweating. I didn't shoot fucking anything except the lock off that pervert's back door. Are you coming with me or not?

What if he doesn't have Ava? What if it was someone else took her? What if she just wandered off on her own?

Wandered off on her own? In her pyjamas and bare feet? You sick fuck. Are you scared? Are you too pussy to come and sort this guy out? I don't want to let Jed hear you saying you're too pussy when he gets back. This is his little girl we're talking about. His precious little baby. Leo sipped from a bottle of warm beer, foam flying down his chin and spattering the front of his sheepskin overcoat.

What are you shouting about Leo? Called Jed. He too was

sweating, panting from his run.

Nothing, just saying that we're going to get Ava back from that pervert. I've blown the lock on the back door, we should go in now.

For Christ's sake Leo, he might have got out now. We'd better go straight in. If he's had the chance to do anything . . . Jed waved his rifle, butt first, at Leo. Sandy, one of the guys from the bar walked slowly behind Jed and deftly removed the weapon from him.

I'm not saying you don't have a right to be upset Jed, but I think there's been enough shooting now.

Jed did not speak, did not turn to face Sandy. Instead he walked towards Daniel's back door and the rest of the group followed. There were murmurs at the back. They'd seen the blue lights. Gray was out searching but he wouldn't have switched them on. It was maybe more than a fox Jed had shot. Some of them thought, but didn't say, that it could even have been little Ava in the trees.

Caroline scraped the ice from the inside of the car as fast as she could. The interior was filled with the smell of anti-freeze and fox fur. Jonny was rocking in the passenger seat, the fox cub curled up on his lap. Caroline hadn't managed to get him out of Ava's robe and he refused to look at her from under the bear hood. The back seat and the boot were full of bags of clothes and toiletries. No photographs, no jewellery, nothing Jed had given her. She suddenly thought. Dismembered Man, Jonny loved it so much. She had to go in and get the comics for him. He'd never forgive her. She laughed, laughed and thought about how silly it was to worry about the comics, but he'd need some comfort from home.

Jonny, I'm going in to get your comics, can you please just sit there quietly. I'll only be a minute. Jonny said nothing. Caroline left the engine running and hoped not too much ice would form before she got back.

Five minutes later, she returned to the car, Jonny was

scraping ice off the windows and the cub was asleep on the floor.

It's nearly all clear now Mummy. Jonny said to Caroline. She didn't like the way he looked at her.

Thank you Jonny, she said as she revved the engine. Can you put your seatbelt on now please?

Sure. Jonny replied and sat back down. Aren't we going to wait for Ava?

Caroline felt sick. She accelerated.

Leo'll look after her now.

Leo?

Daddy. I meant Daddy's going to look after her. We've got to go.

Jonny looked blankly at Caroline. His eyes closed. Even in the bitter cold of the speeding car he fell fast asleep. Shock probably, blood loss. The fox cub slept too, nuzzling against Jonny's feet. Thank God it was only a baby. The older ones would be tearing the attic up by now. Jed's fault. Leo's fault. Her fault too.

As Caroline drove across the valley she could see blue lights tailing off into the distance. The strip club was in darkness though. A bad sign. But the house next door, the strange man's house, was blazing with light. She knew what they'd be saying, what they'd be doing. But it wasn't his fault. She drove towards the lights.

Daniel was curled up behind his sofa. The pile of bones in his hands. If they saw them, if they'd left them, he was in trouble. He couldn't be seen with tiny bones just now. He'd seen enough burning piles of foxes over the winter to know where they came from. Every day, following a cull, the bodies lay in heaps, pelts singed, bones shining through, the fire tinged with green as strange smells leaked into the air. A heavy scent of barbecued meat and then the chemicals of decay. Sometimes, if there was a lot of shot, it gleamed at the last, molten silver balls lay glowing amongst the remains.

These men were not peaceful, these men who came to his house. And the odour of cherry soap was still on his hands.

What are you doing? Caroline screamed. She'd parked the car round the corner and left it running. She couldn't see Jed or Leo but knew they must be amongst the rest of the men.

Caroline, there's no call for you to be here, we're dealing with this. Sandy said.

Dealing with what? This man hasn't done anything.

Jed came out, following the sound of his wife's voice.

What is it Caroline? He said, softly.

Get Leo out here too.

Look Caroline, you just go back home, we'll sort this out. He's done nothing wrong, you know he hasn't.

Do you want me to call Gray? I'll get him to take you home.

What have you done to him?

Big Chris walked over to Caroline; put his hand on her shoulder. Go home, the minute we find anything out we'll let you know.

Will you? Like you let me know about the silver dress? Big Chris looked confused at this outburst. Jed came forward.

What is it? What do you want?

She's dead isn't she? You know it and Leo knows it and you're doing all this to that poor man. There's nothing I can do. You're going to torture that poor man and Gray's going to make sure you get the chance.

You're hysterical. Calm down.

I wouldn't let anything happen to her Caroline, you know that. It was Leo from the doorway.

I just bet you wouldn't. Caroline replied. Before anyone had a chance to say any more she started to run, climbed into the waiting car and accelerated across the ice. Jonny woke up for a second, then settled back down to sleep.

24 DECEMBER 0500

Forked Bone Cup
Appearance: White cups with blue 'X-ray'-like veins
Effects: Attacks bone and muscle.
Environment: Near Plums and Custard

Lou, Lou. The doctor is going to put a tube in to your mouth now, is there anything you want to tell us first.

Leave her alone, she hasn't done anything, why are you here Gray?

Detective Madden, sweetheart.

Yeah well it wasn't Detective Madden last night in the club was it? You were Gray then you bastard. Ginny's face was so angry that the dusting of glitter on her nose looked impossibly silly. Gray ignored her remark and roughly pushed her aside.

There are witnesses here; you can't do that you bastard. Clara said in Gray's ear. Get away from Lou, she needs attention. Is it her fault she was shot?

You tell me sweetheart. What was she doing out there? I thought you girls said she was too drunk and you'd sent her home. She doesn't look too drunk to me. Gray raised his arm to Clara but she was ahead of him, she ducked away and pulled the emergency cord. Two male nurses arrived.

You're all going to have to leave now. This is unacceptable. How many of you dancing girls are there? One said.

Look, I need to get some information from this woman before you do anything to her.

Before we do anything to her? I am going to have to ask you to vacate the area Detective, and come back when this girl is in a fit state. She's barely conscious, what kind of information can you hope to get from her like that?

Listen here, you know who I am, you know what's been going on tonight, we need to know where the little girl is.

What little girl? Clara asked.

Oh, you didn't know? I'm looking for Ava; she's been missing for hours.

How would Lou know where she is?

You tell me.

The two nurses closed the curtains around Lou and Gray Madden, Clara and Ginny found themselves alone on the outside.

Come on sweets, let's go and wait somewhere else. We'll be here when she comes round. If he's waiting then so are we, said Clara

So you go to a lot of these pageants then Daniel? Jed asked. He seemed genuinely interested.

No. I mean, I've been to a few but not as many as you. Daniel replied. He was feeling confused, the men had seemed violent when they'd come in, but now they were sitting quietly on the sofas, letting the man who'd introduced himself as Jed do all the talking. There were about seven of them, and the big one, the one he knew had been responsible for the letters on his workshop, he paced around the group occasionally, holding them back. He hadn't expected it, for that red faced drunk to be keeping everyone calm.

What are you saying there Daniel? You saying there's something wrong with me going to my daughter's pageants? Jed didn't sound any different but the words weren't friendly.

No, no I mean I don't have the same cause to go, that's all.

Not the same cause. What is your cause? Mine is to support my little girl, my daughter. What is it that you're doing exactly? Looking at little girls, drawing pictures of them in your sick little sketchbook?

Daniel began to shake slightly. His arm trembled so much that it began to bounce against the back of the sofa. These kinds of words he'd heard before.

Why did you come here? It's late, I'm tired. It's Christmas. He looked at the room and felt nothing. It had become a safe place for him for a while, but they were going to take it away from him. He didn't think he could bear it any longer if that enormously fat one didn't take his arm off Magdalena. He jumped up. Rushed the fat man.

Get off her, she doesn't like being handled.

The fat man looked amazed. The others didn't say anything for a minute, and then the red faced one dashed from the other side of the room; he picked Daniel up and slammed him into a wall before he could understand what was going on.

Doesn't like being handled? It's a fucking sex doll. It doesn't have any feelings. What is wrong with you? You care about this piece of plastic but you don't care about hurting a young girl!

I didn't hurt her. Daniel said before he saw Leo's fist coming towards his head.

The grey-haired male nurse came to speak to Ginny and Clara in the waiting room, much friendlier than he had been before.

Hi girls, she's feeling a bit better now. It wasn't quite as bad as I said; I just wanted to get that prick off her case. We've removed the bullet and cleaned her up. It was just a graze to her arm but she'll need to be on antibiotics and pain relief for a while. We need to keep her in, but you can go and visit with her for a few minutes. I'll tell him that she's under anaesthetic and he should come back another day.

Thanks, Clara said, he is a prick.

What about the bullet though, are you going to test who

shot it?

What do you think happened? A lot of guys out 'hunting', he rolled his eyes at the absurdity of this, and a girl happens to get shot. And you think the likes of Madden is going to do something about it? Do yourselves a favour and your friend, keep out of their way and get out of town.

But it's our town too, why should they have it because they're stronger than us?

They're not stronger, Ginny said to Clara, Girl they're weak. Weak as milk. But there are a lot of them and there are hardly any of us. You think that prick Madden is anything but a pussy, he's scared shitless one of our parties is going to get back to his wife. When someone is a terrible coward, they lash out and they cover up. And we can get hurt by that or not. Lou's been shot, something awful's happened to Ava and no one's going to do anything about it.

Look, I sympathise, I do, but I'm not going to get mixed up with these people either. All I want to do is get on with my work.

Can you at least keep the bullet for us though? And then if there is anything we can do?

Okay, I'll keep the bullet for you, I'll send it to the laboratory anonymously and I'll tell Madden we couldn't get it all out.

Thanks.

Yeah thanks, you're a real hero.

Clara, Ginny said as the nurse walked away, sometimes you don't know when to shut the fuck up.

Well thanks for your support.

Okay, you're upset, let's not get too heated over this. We need to go and speak to Lou and be all bright and smiling and then see if we can find out anything about Ava.

Okay Ginny. Sorry. Clara said, a tear rolling through her bear eye make-up.

The girls held hands and walked in to see their friend.

When Daniel woke up he couldn't see anything but the bottom of a boot. He could smell polish and leather and animal faeces.

Ughhh! He said. The boot pressed down on his face, gently, but it was hard for him to breathe. It tasted like shit, like meat dust. He rebelled. There was a wet thunking noise as he pushed his tongue out. The sound he made did not mean what he wanted it to. It meant he was scared, he was messy. It meant he was undignified.

The boot came away and Daniel was yanked up under his armpits by the red faced man, he was on the sofa and there was no one else in the room but the two of them. The fire was on, and it was too hot. Too bright. He was sweating and his lower back hurt where he had been manhandled.

Who are you? He said and the red faced man seemed keen to talk. He was that kind of man, someone who enjoyed an audience. Daniel intuited this but he didn't think it would help him.

Who am I? I'm that little girl's daddy.

What? Daniel was confused. He thought the other one was Ava's father.

Only you're not going to tell anyone that are you? You would have no call to piss me off right now would you?

Could I have a glass of water? I feel funny.

There's a glass in the kitchen. It's got cherry lip balm smeared all over the rim. Where is she Daniel?

She's not here. I don't know.

Well those six men out there will soon find out if she is. They thought I'd probably manage you in here on my own.

Where are the girls?

The girls? You mean the sex dolls? Is that the kind of thing you show a little girl?

They're my friends. Daniel said. He knew there was nothing good going to happen now; he didn't want to betray them. There was no reason to.

Where is she Daniel? Asked Leo, running a knife blade

slowly across his coat sleeve, wiping it until it shone.

What's going on Lou? Clara knew she shouldn't ask, but she couldn't help it.

I'm sorry girls. I didn't mean it to happen.

Why did you get shot?

I was following Jed and Leo and Chris, I had to tell Bob what they were doing.

But you were too drunk to stand.

I wasn't, I needed an excuse to get away. I'm sorry; I didn't mean all this to happen.

Do you know where Ava is?

What?

Ava, you know, the cute little girl from the pageant? Apparently she's missing.

Bob . . . started Lou and then the painkiller stopped her speaking any more, she fell soundly asleep.

Bob. Said Ginny.

Yes? Said Bob as he walked into the room.

25 DECEMBER 0600

Frosted Cap
Appearance: Sparkly black cups, thin stem.
Effects: Dizzyness and euphoria
Environment: Deep valleys

So she's not here then? Leo asked for the tenth time.

No Leo she'd not here, Jed replied. She's not anywhere in the house.

Nowhere?

Yeah, I told you.

Where are his *girls*? Leo leered.

The dolls?

Yeah, the dolls.

Upstairs.

Right.

Chris! Leo shouted. Bring the dolls downstairs.

Daniel squirmed under Leo's boot. It rested, lightly, on his stomach.

Don't do anything to the girls. He swallowed, please.

What did you say?

Please don't do anything to the girls. I didn't do anything to your little girl.

What the fuck did you say? Jed brought his face right up to Daniel's. Whose little girl?

Leo took his boot off Daniel's stomach and stood back, he

thought he should let Jed get whatever off his chest with the faggot. He went out to find Big Chris and the dolls. Their stupidly round mouths and unnaturally bright eyes unnerved him. He wanted them dead. He laughed when he thought that, how could they be dead? They were fuckdolls. He'd been up too many hours and his thinking was shot.

Look, you leave them there at the bottom of the stairs Chris; I'll sort them out in a minute. I'm going to see if he has any liquor worth shit. Why don't you check the treehouse? It's the only place left to look.

How am I supposed to get up there?

I don't fucking know, climb, whatever.

Alright, but you better save me a drink.

Thanks Chris.

Leo was conscious of leaving Jed alone with Daniel, if there was one thing bound to rile him up it was talking to that sick creep about Ava. And he needed Jed onside when the fire started. He didn't want to have to argue with him at this time of night. It wouldn't be long until dawn and he'd had a bellyful of it all by now. Sleep, he needed, and plenty of it. Leo walked to the kitchen and found a bottle of gin.

What the fuck? He said to himself. A faggot's drink. It would do though. He was measuring it into mugs when Big Chris came back inside and started shouting.

Jed, you've got to come see this.

Chris, he hissed, leave Jed alone, why're you telling him?

It's his little girl.

She's out there? In the treehouse?

No, but there's a lot of weird shit out there and a little pile of blond hair.

What?

There's a pile of blond hair that looks like Ava's in the treehouse with some fox fur and some silver material, it's all laid out, arranged. It's not normal. We should tell Gray.

No, let me have a look first. Leo put down the gin and walked quickly out to the yard.

Bob didn't take off his sheepskin coat as he sat down in the chair next to Lou's bed. She began to moan quietly as he placed his hand over her mouth, resting gently. He began talking, as though he wasn't choking her with his leather glove.

Poor thing looks in bad shape. Whatever they've given her she seems to be raving. I saw her earlier, in the bar, you girls think I don't notice anything but I saw the state she was in. champagne, cocktails, coke. And then whatever the fuck is in this drip. You think she's going to be coherent?

Bob, Clara said, could you take your hand off her mouth please?

Bob laughed, made as though he didn't realize what he had been doing. He placed his hand in his lap. Resting just as gently.

I think the police want to talk to you Bob.

Yeah I saw Gray out there, told him what I could. I think he wants to see the two of you now. Don't worry; I'll keep an eye on Lou while you're gone. Don't want anything else happening to my girls. 'Specially tonight. I didn't leave my poor wife at home with Cherry and Molly on Christmas Eve for nothing did I? He smiled at them, his blue-white dentures translucent in the blast of hospital light.

Stay there, Ginny said to Clara, I'll be one minute. She stood up and walked out of the room. Clara pushed her chair forward so she could sit between Lou and Bob. She didn't look at him as she spoke.

Bob, Lou already told us what happened. We're not going to talk to Gray Madden, we're going to talk to the real police. It would be best if you left now. Go home to your wife and your girls. You maybe should appreciate this Christmas together.

Clarissa, Bob started.

You know my name, prick.

Whatever. You know that I'm all for everyone having their

fun during the holidays, but what are you talking about? You think that the 'real police' are going to talk to a couple of whores about how there was some big conspiracy and that's why their coked up friend got herself shot? Yeah, I think you misunderstood how the system works a little bit.

Clara said nothing. She squeezed Lou's hand.

Right, Ginny said as she returned to the room, I spoke to Gray. He does want to speak to us but he's agreed to do it in here. I told him we'd be happier staying with Lou for now, but we want to help if we can, with Ava.

Clara was so angry she could barely lift her head. Why should they speak to Gray? He wouldn't help them. But there was no other way to stop Bob being on his own with Lou. She looked at the cord. Thought of the nurse who came earlier. But if he didn't come again, if it was someone else they might just send her and Ginny away.

That's very kind of you Gray. She said.

It's Detective Madden, Clara.

It's Miss Kendrick in that case, she replied, a little too sharply.

Fine, Miss Kendrick, Gray did not seem to notice her tone.

Bob? Bob? They went to Daniel's house and they shot the fox. The fox's blood went all over me. I don't know what happened. Bob? Did you hear me?

Oh my God! Clara squeezed Lou's hand tighter. Don't upset yourself sweetie, it's Clara. Don't worry about Bob, Bob's here too and he's not mad at you. Are you Bob?

Get some rest Lou, don't try to talk, you don't know what you're saying.

Lou sat upright suddenly and Clara tried to keep the drip positioned in her hand so she didn't hurt herself.

Clara. Why're you here? Ginny?

You were hurt Lou, when the fox got shot, you got shot too.

You bastard Bob, why did you let me do something so dangerous? You knew that might happen. What did you do with Ava? I don't want anything to happen to her.

Bob, you know where Ava is?

Clara, we'd better leave. Ginny was grabbing her arm.

Leave? Clara raised her voice, shook Ginny off.

We can't help Ava here.

We can't leave Lou.

I'm going to get the nurse; we need to clear this room.

Fine, get the nurse but don't leave her here with these two creeps.

Clara, we're going to get arrested.

You certainly will Miss Kendrick if you cause any more fuss.

Any more fuss? Ava's missing and Lou's been shot because of this man.

Gray Madden removed his gun from his hip and ran it, slowly, along his gloved palm.

Now there have been a lot of allegations here, and this man's good name has been attacked. On top of that there have been allegations of illegal drug taking and attempted violence from all three of you girls. I can handcuff every one of you, shot or not shot, and I can take all means necessary to restrain you if you get out of hand. Or you can leave, quietly, and I can get on with my job.

Don't leave me. Lou said quietly, her eyes full of tears.

Clara pulled the emergency cord and the sound of a siren filled the room. Within seconds the male nurse arrived with two other men. One was dressed in an orderly's uniform, the other in white scrubs.

Could you clear the area please?

This woman is under arrest, I need to stay here.

No she isn't, you didn't arrest her, Clara said.

Please leave, all of you, I need to attend to this woman and if you don't clear the area you may be party to attempted murder.

You know nothing about the law, Gray said. You're talking shit.

I have four witnesses, one of whom is a surgeon at the city

hospital. Do you want to take the risk?

Gray, we can sort this out tomorrow, she's not going any-where. Bob appealed to his friend.

Gray said nothing but spat at the floor. He followed Bob out of the room, the gun still in his hand.

Go and wait in the toilet outside, the orderly whispered to Clara and Ginny, I'll escort you, I'll lock the front doors and you can come back in here. I'm not letting you two go out there with what's going on tonight.

Thanks, whispered Clara. She and Ginny followed him out of the room.

Look, Leo said to the other guys. There's no point you being here anymore. You go home, it's Christmas. Me and Jed can take it from here.

You sure Leo? You don't want us to do anything?

Can you bring the dolls through to the living room? I figure it's a way to make him talk.

Gives me the creeps the way he seems to be in love with those dolls.

Yeah, well. Leo said.

Doesn't it give you the creeps Leo?

Chris, I asked you to do something; then I asked you to go home. Can you be a good boy and do that for me? Please?

Alright Leo. Big Chris walked back to the house to do what Leo asked. Leo climbed back up to the treehouse. He took a handkerchief out of his pocket and placed the blonde hair, fox fur and silver dress inside it; then he folded it up and replaced it in his jacket. He poured the liquor from the mush-rooms out of the window and ground the mushrooms under-foot. The frayed rope, cut from the ladder, he bunched up and stuffed in his pocket next to the handkerchief. He jumped back down from the treehouse and walked back to the house.

Where have you been? asked Jed.

I found these out in the treehouse, said Leo, he laid out the handkerchief.

What the hell is that? Daniel asked.

I think you know don't you? How did you find out about the parties?

What? What parties?

You're joking right. The silver dress, the fox fur, the mushrooms.

I don't understand. What are you talking about?

Look Leo, it doesn't matter. We just need to get Ava back. Jed had tears in his eyes. Just tell me where she is. I'll let you go, we won't hurt you.

He'll hurt me anyway. Daniel said. Leo felt warm when he said that, a blush rose on his cheek and he had to smile. Daniel was a smart cookie. Too smart.

I might not hurt you. Leo said. But I think I'm going to have a bit of fun with these dolls.

What? No, leave them alone. At least . . .

At least what Daniel?

At least leave Magdalena and Lucy alone.

Oh, I see, it comes down to that does it? You care about them. But not the others. Now Leo had his face right up close to Daniel's. He felt foolish for respecting him. The loyalty he'd shown was not authentic. He did not offer to go in their place. There was nothing that this man could tell them.

Jed, make sure he doesn't move.

Leo walked to the sofa, where the dolls had been piled up. All he wanted was to get rid of their faces; the faces were the worst part. He took a lighter out of his pocket and opened it so the flame was high. He threw it on to the tangle of bodies. But they did not burn.

You can hurt them but you can't kill them. They're realflesh,

What? Leo asked. This was getting spooky. What do you mean I can't kill them? They're not alive.

No but they're realflesh. It doesn't burn.

Well you'll burn pretty well instead.

No, Jed said, we need to know where Ava is.

Jed, Leo said to his friend, putting his arm on his shoulder. Ava's dead. He's not going to tell us anything. And he knows too much.

What? Jed blinked, threw Leo's hand off his shoulder.

Come on, he knows about the mushroom parties. He knows what happened to that girl. He warned us.

I don't know, I don't know anything.

Now Jed, I want you to calm down. I'm going to throw this lighter at the gas stove and we're going to run, real fast, away from here. Now I don't want you to get hurt so you have to run.

Jed looked at Leo, tears still in his eyes. The coating on the realflesh was singeing and the room was filling with toxic smoke.

I thought they wouldn't burn Daniel?

You don't understand what I've been saying. Daniel spoke gently.

Leo grabbed Jed's shoulders firmly and threw the open flame on to the gas stove. He pushed Jed towards the front door and out of the house. They ran as fast as they could across the snow as the sky began to flash red and toxic smoke billowed across the valley.

24 DECEMBER 0700

Smoky Polypore
Appearance: Smoke-coloured fronds.
Effects: Edible, used for preserving meat.
Environment: Harbours, beaches, seafronts.

Jed and Leo coughed as the smoke filled their lungs. They said nothing as they walked across the valley, said nothing and didn't look back. Leo had Ava's hair in his pocket; he touched it as he walked. The hair felt tough, springy. It wasn't soft like a baby's hair should be.

Why did you dye her hair Jed?

What? What are you saying to me? You're now taking an interest in her hair? You're a vicious bastard Leo; you never gave a shit about her before. Not when the cash was right.

Yeah, well a baby's hair is soft; her hair's like chicken wire.

Jed said nothing.

Leo could hear the sound of the fire crackling behind him, the smell of plastic was getting stronger, he felt sick.

She was a baby Jed. Just a little baby. Leo felt his voice shake. He was unhappy but the sickness was stronger, if he couldn't shake off the nausea he felt he'd have to lie down.

Going to rest a minute Jed.

Leo fell forward and vomited. It wasn't a bad feeling. The crisp snow absorbed the alcoholic bile and he felt empty.

The cold felt good on his face, his arms. He heaved again and when no more vomit came out he felt rested. There was nothing left to worry about. Leo curled up into a ball and smiled.

Leo. Get up. Jed covered his mouth with his scarf. The smoke was so pungent it was making him dizzy. We've got to leave, it's dangerous.

I'm fine here Jed. It's okay.

Jed bent down and hooked his arms around Leo's waist and hoisted him up. Leo took the hair out of his pocket and passed it to Jed.

You should have it.

Jed took the hair and scattered it on the ground. He put his arm around Leo and helped him to walk. A few blond strands stuck to his gloved fingertips as they made their slow way home.

Lou could see sweat running along Clara's arms, there was something wrong with her face, it looked purple, bruised. Lou couldn't understand why her hands were cupped around a grey bowl. Lou was too confused to do anything but let her mouth hang open and allow Clara to spoon something sweet inside it. Lou could see the red blur of Ginny's hair in the corner. She was covered in something silver and sparkling.

Ginny you look so beautiful. The room is sad but you are so shiny.

Lou didn't know if she had said that because the spoon was still in her mouth and no one spoke back to here. Ginny had her head bent, reading something maybe, or sleeping in the chair. There was a flash of white in her hand too. An unlit cigarette? A cigarette would be perfect now, Lou thought. No more of this sweet stuff, a cigarette and a cold glass of something.

Ughhh! Lou was surprised when the spoon went in again; there was a worse taste. Lou saw that it wasn't Clara pushing the spoon into her mouth but a man. A tall man in a white uniform.

Perhaps they will come back, thought Lou.

Yes, they're just outside for a minute while I sort you out. You can talk to them briefly, said the nurse.

Lou was surprised. She didn't know she had spoken. She was pleased that she had though, pleased that the girls would be coming back. The curtain had been drawn and the sky was pale pink, but it frightened Lou, a line of blood red scarred the horizon. Fire, Lou thought, there is a fire.

Nurse! She said, but the sound would not come.

Brrrrr! Lou shivered when the sheet was taken off her. The man in the white uniform put something cold on Lou's head and placed a thin sheet over her shoulders. He drew off her blood soaked dress slowly, gently. Cool water swept over Lou's damp flesh and the sharp smells of blood and sweat were replaced with soap. He towelled Lou like a baby, patting her skin dry and she felt so peaceful under his fingers. He sprinkled her with powder and eased her up to help her into a paper gown.

Now you can see your friends. The man said.

The truck's gone. Leo said.

Yeah.

She must have been serious.

Yeah.

I don't blame her.

You don't blame her? I blame you.

Yeah, well what's the point of it now? We did what we wanted.

We need to find Ava.

Ava? You think that there's anything left of her to find?

What do you mean?

Jed unlocked the door.

Shh, what's that sound?

Both men stopped and listened.

Ava. Jed said. It's Ava's voice.

The cry became louder and sharper as they walked inside. A wounded, painful sound. Leo pushed Jed out of the way and walked to the foot of the stairs. Since he'd been sick outside he felt like he could do anything. He ran all the way up, towards the sound. He knew that she must have been in her room all the time, she'd probably been there, all wrapped up in bed and now she was confused because everyone had left her. Leo would go and find her now though, and give her all the love in the world. There was no one else to look after her. No one could ruin things now, not Daniel or Caroline or that little prick Jonny. But she wasn't in her room, the door was open and there was no one there. The sound was coming from somewhere higher. From his room, upstairs. She must have known that he was the only person she could trust, not any of the other bastards. He climbed the second set of stairs, walking towards his little girl.

Leo! Leo! Jed shouted, he ran up the stairs, if Leo opened the attic door and the foxes came out they'd have no chance. He was totally out of it and he didn't know what he was doing.

Leo.

Leo turned round and spoke to Jed. Leave her alone, she doesn't want you. I'll look after her.

No, it's not Ava, listen it's the foxes. Caroline must have done something to upset them. They sound mad. Don't open the fucking door, come back downstairs.

No Jed, it's my turn to look after her now, you didn't look after her. Just go away. She's mine.

Leo. Jed screamed. He considered grabbing Leo's legs and dragging him back down the stairs. But in this mood he had too much strength.

She's down here. Jed said, I saw her down here.

Leo looked at Jed when he said that, a slow smile coming. What?

Ava's downstairs. In the basement.

Playing?

Yeah, Jed was sweating as he spoke, his face a mess, yeah she's playing.

Ava's playing in the basement.

Jed could hear the foxes screeching now; they could tell the men were in the house. What had Caroline done? A fear went through Jed as he thought of the little one, the baby. Jonny had been playing with it earlier and maybe something had happened. If he'd hurt the cub then the vixen would want to kill them. If Leo opened the door.

We're coming baby. Shouted Jed down the stairs. Daddy's here.

Leo turned around; the key in his hand fell out.

I'm coming Ava, baby. Leo said and he followed Jed downstairs.

Lou, how are you?

How do you think Clara? She looks like shit.

Ginny? Were you just sitting over there with a cigarette?

No smoking in here Lou, it's a hospital. I was sitting over there but we had to get rid of that prick Gray Madden and Bob too.

Bob! Where is he? He'll kill me. Lou tried to sit up and started grabbing at the needle taped to her hand.

Lou, it's okay, Clara said.

Listen Lou, Ginny said as she firmly took Lou's hands. If you want us to stay in here you're going to have to calm down. Bob and Madden are out of the way, the front door is bolted and the nurse is outside. We can have a quick chat and then you have to sleep. If I take my hands away will you settle down?

Yes. Lou said.

Because if you don't, Ginny's going to pump a sedative into you. Clara laughed, then stopped.

Okay, I got confused. It's okay now. It wasn't Bob that shot me though, you know that right?

We don't know anything.

Oh god I'm so sorry, I deserved to get shot. I shouldn't have tried to mess around on both sides. I didn't tell Bob though, I swear it wasn't me. He found out about the parties and he wanted to know what they were doing. He said he gave them enough already, with the pageants, why did they need the extra?

Well it's fair enough, anyone can make money.

Yeah but he wanted to be part of it. Ava's been winning pageants all over the country thanks to his connections. And then Jed and Leo were using her as an attraction, to get people to their filthy parties.

No they weren't, the parties have nothing to do with Ava.

What?

They have nothing to do with her; we just hand out drinks and let everyone get stoned on mushrooms. It's the mushrooms people come for, not Ava. What, did you really think we'd get involved in that?

I don't understand. He said he was going to kidnap Ava, he said she was his. He thought he could show them he was boss and get more publicity for the pageants.

So where is she then?

I don't know, I went to get her earlier, but she was gone.

What do you mean? She was gone?

I mean someone must have been there before me because her bed was empty.

But you were so drunk earlier.

Of course I wasn't. Everyone thought I went home but I went to the house, I crept in through the bathroom window and went upstairs, Jonny was asleep and Caroline was too drunk to notice. But she'd gone already. I thought Bob had her. But when I went to meet him, and told him he said he hadn't seen her and told me to go and follow the men, he didn't know what they were up to but he sure as shit didn't think it was fox hunting. He told me they kept foxes in the attic, it was their fault they're getting so big and wild and it's so they can cover up their strange games.

Lou, said Ginny, I think you need to rest now.

Lou was already falling asleep. Just to be on the safe side, Ginny called the nurse to give her a sedative.

She looks tired as all hell, said the nurse.

Yeah, she was rambling a bit towards the end but we still don't know what happened to Ava.

It's not your responsibility to find her, leave it to the police.

You just seen who the police are, shouted Clara.

I mean the county police. I've already called them, they're on the way.

Clara said nothing.

Ginny thanked the nurse, kissed Lou on the head and steered Clara towards the door.

Bedtime. She said.

Merry Christmas, said the nurse.

Clara laughed.

Leo was walking so fast down the stairs that he stumbled at the bottom and fell flat out in the hallway. Jed sat him up, leaning against the wall.

Leo, listen to me, you're not feeling very well. It's been a bad night and you haven't slept in a long time. You need to sit still and calm down for a while.

Ava? He asked, quietly, knowing the answer.

Ava's dead Leo. You know that. She's gone.

But we got the bastard, we got him, burned him, burned him up didn't we.

I'm going to pack a bag and then we're going to leave for a while.

Leave?

Bob's not going to stand for this, you know that.

He doesn't know about the parties.

Then why was that girl following us?

You think he knows? Leo looked focused for a second, his eyes fixed on Jed.

I think he's known for some time, and if that girl's not dead then he'll have proof.

We've got to get out of here.

Leo looked like he was about to struggle up off the ground.

I'll get some clothes and help you out to the car. You can have a sleep for a couple of hours, but that's about all I've got left in me. You'll have to sober up by then.

25 DECEMBER 0800

Amethyst Deceiver
Appearance: Shades of purple and blue. Big umbrella-like cup.
Effects: Safe and edible. Antidote to Destroying Angels.
Environment: Near Destroying Angels .

We should go see if he needs help, Clara said, looking over at the flames.

Clara, don't be ridiculous, the wood's starting to buckle. That fire's been going a long time, maybe the whole time we've been in the hospital. He's either outside, or he's dead.

But we should go and check.

You check if you want, me, I'm going to get out from this toxic smoke and get to my bed.

Clara knew Ginny was right, the smoke was thick and tinged with green. There was poison pouring through the sky. The whole place was desolate. Some Christmas morning.

Ginny, Clara began, the smoke was hurting her lungs and it was a minute before she could continue. Where are the fire trucks? It wasn't what she had intended to say, but suddenly, she realized, it was what she wanted to know.

I'm sure they're coming. Ginny seemed dazed, tired.

When I get home I'll call them, just to make sure, thought Clara.

Ginny, Clara said again.

What? Ginny replied.

Why didn't you tell Lou the truth?

What? What do you mean the truth?

You said that the parties were just about mushrooms.

They were.

Partly, but that wasn't all.

Listen Clara, you're a good girl and you've been a great help to all of us, but I don't think you're that smart. Sometimes, in fact, you're pretty stupid.

But we can trust Lou, she told us about Bob.

She told us nothing, except that she'd lied to us before. She told us this when raving on morphine. D'you think that it would be sensible to feed her more information, just in time for Bob and Gray to get back and interrogate her some more?

Clara felt suddenly dizzy. Ginny was right, they couldn't trust Lou at all.

Look, the only reason I wanted to stay was to see how much she knew. And if they come back, they'll find out we said nothing.

The smoke began to clear a little as a gust of wind thinned it out, and Clara reached out in front of her, as if to grasp the cleaner air. Her hand looked so pale against the green sky, she thought she might faint. She didn't want Ginny to know something was wrong, so she feigned a coughing fit, thinking what to do next.

Will you help Lou testify against Bob, I mean if it comes to it?

Testify what? That he wanted Ava kidnapped?

Yeah. I mean, if she hadn't been gone, and Lou had handed her over . . .

Then what? He would have looked after her. He would have treated her like a princess.

Did you know about this? Clara asked Ginny. Her whole body was glittering in the green haze and she looked as fierce and terrible as an icon.

Ginny rolled her eyes. You are a very stupid girl aren't you?

You think you're special, and different and arty but you're no good. You're uppity and you're in your own little world. Of course I knew about it. But it doesn't matter. You didn't know, and Lou didn't know and she got shot not me.

So she was never supposed to find Ava?

No, she was supposed to tell everyone she hadn't found Ava. That the kidnap plot had failed.

Then, where's Ava?

Back home. Where I left her.

You?

Yes, when you were dancing and Lou was out following Jed and Leo. I met Bob at the treehouse and took her back home.

But I don't understand.

We wanted to show them that it could be done. That they needed to stop taking risks and making money both ways. And I don't care what you say, those children shouldn't have been treated the way they were.

What do you mean? Clara could think only of Ava, she had to go and check on her, she had to get away from Ginny. The smoke was beginning to drift over more thickly again and she could hear the sounds of the wood splintering under the strain of the heat. If she started to run, it would be hard for Ginny to spot her.

Yeah, said Clara.

You know they keep wild foxes in that house? She wasn't really rambling, it's their fault. They've been breeding them up in the attic, drugging them and letting them loose. With children in the house.

Why? Clara couldn't help asking.

Fox 'culls' they call them, part of the entertainment we offer in the valley. You and me are another type of sport. And you know how those parties got out of hand.

But they weren't meant to.

Weren't they?

Suddenly Clara was sick of Ginny's whole cynical, black-hearted shtick.

Don't just say that, say what you mean, unless you don't know either?

They were feeding mushrooms to the kids as well, so's they didn't know what was going on, and if they ever asked any difficult questions it could just be put down to the weird dreams they were having. Bob didn't hold with that and neither did I.

Bastards. Clara was crying now, she didn't want to know anymore.

Oh and I guess you think you're no worse than the rest of us? Ginny said. Are you without blame? You held Ava's hand and made her look away when that girl died.

Oh shit, thought Clara, Ginny thinks she's got that over me, she thinks that's going to keep me quiet. I've got a chance.

You're right Ginny. You're right. I took money from them all as well. We're the same. Clara was sweating now, hoping Ginny wouldn't see. She thought of Ava and knew she could get away. She'd take Ava, go and find Lou and they could all explain what had happened. She'd go to the house and find her, but what if Jed and Leo stopped her or what if?

Yes, we're the same.

The smoke darkened the air; Clara dipped low on the ground and ran, on all fours, as fast as she could. Her ears were pinned back by the wind and her hands, in bear mittens, were still stung by the snow.

How funny, she thought, I really will be kidnapping Ava this time.

By the time Clara arrived at Ava's house she was exhausted. The air was not so thick on that side of the valley but her lungs burned with effort all the same. The car was gone and so was Leo's truck. No lights in the house. Clara saw a small window open a crack on the side of the house. Her hands were still cold but she managed to push the window further down with the heels of both palms. It would be a squeeze but she wasn't wearing very much. Clara put her head inside first, to see if she could hear anything. There was a single cry, a child's cry. She didn't think about it any longer but pushed herself down onto her hands into the black space.

Ugh. She said as she twisted her body through the window. She carefully moved her hands forwards and slid onto her stomach. As her feet followed she tightened into a ball, not knowing where she was or how much room she had. There was a musty smell in the room, slightly sweet. There were no more cries and Clara couldn't hear anyone else in the house. She found the wall with her hands and shifted round so her back was against it. Bone by bone, she stood up slowly and reached out her hands until she found a light pull. The bare light bulb above her head came on and in her surprise she hit her head against it. The bulb began to swing and threw long shadows across the room. Clara looked down and gasped. She was at the top of a set of stone stairs, inches from falling all the way to the bottom. The light was making her feel dizzy and she stilled it with her hand. There was a door at the top of the stairs, but it had been locked. Holding on to the rail, Clara made her way down to the bottom of the stairs.

At first, Clara did not recognise Ava. There was a small, bald child lying on the stone slab at the bottom of the stairs. Ava wasn't bald, she had blond hair. But the child was wearing a pink peignoir that she had seen Ava wear. The bald child had blood at the corner of her mouth and purple marks on her throat. The room was full of mannequins, and there were legs, arms, heads abandoned all over the floor. Some of the mannequins wore party dresses, evening gowns, negligees. All of them were the same size as the child. Perhaps, thought Clara, perhaps that is a mannequin too, perhaps that is not a child. And she walked to the stone slab and touched the paper lantern skin of the doll, stretched across her collarbones. And the skin was cold, but as soon as she touched it, a purple snowflake appeared beneath her fingertips as blood spread and pooled. Clara thought that she would scream, because the bald child was dead and she was wearing Ava's clothes. But she didn't scream, she climbed up on to the slab instead and put her arms around Ava's waist, and lay quietly with her. The cries began again and it was when she heard growling that Clara remembered the foxes.

PART FOUR: PLAYING DEAD

2100 1 OCTOBER

2100 1 OCTOBER

The woman in the silver dress wouldn't stop screaming. She had been told what to expect, what was coming, but still she wouldn't stop.

Clara spoke to Ginny softly. Couldn't we talk to them?

No. we can't get involved.

But I don't think she understood what it would be like.

She understood the money.

But why do they have to burn her?

Because they like it. Because they've paid for the privilege.

But the kids are here.

They don't know what's going on.

But I think they do.

They're next door.

They're acting strange, like maybe they accidentally ate some of the mushrooms or something.

Yeah well, these guys wouldn't be here if Ava wasn't.

But, you're not serious, they wouldn't do that.

No. It's all worded very carefully. They pay to come and have sex. At the same party that the kids are at. If they add two and two and make five, that's their problem.

But it's dangerous.

Ginny rolled her eyes. You're on.

What? I've done my bit.

You have to burn her with cigarettes now.

Clara looked at Ginny, terrified.

Joke.

Clara laughed, tried to smile.

I'm just going to look in on the kids.

Yeah, you do that Mary Poppins.

Clara could still hear the woman in the silver dress whimpering, but she seemed calmer. Clara hated the whole night, the men biting her and calling her a whore but it was nothing, nothing to watching the colour this girl was turning under the harsh yellow bulb. There had been blood on her face and she had turned nearly green with fear and pain. It was a shame, Clara thought, that there wasn't a better industry in the valley. If you were smart you wanted to leave, and if you wanted to leave you had to make money, and if you were a girl there was only one way to do that. Clara would rather do ten parties than one hundred dances. She wished she could explain that to the weeping woman. And she wished she could tell her that the stronger you were the more they left you alone. Crying only prolonged it. She still felt sick to think of the way the kids were being used. They were underground in the prison, and it only took one angry customer to get out of hand. There was no way anyone would get here in time. She shivered, and pulled her wrap around her shoulders, glad she'd got her spot over with.

Ava? Jonny? Where are you?

Clara couldn't see either of the children, and they didn't respond to her shouting. She thought maybe they'd wandered into the main room and walked back the way she'd come.

Clara, could you get her out of here please?

What?

There's going to be someone to meet you at the gates. She had some sort of seizure and there's nothing to be done so could you carry her out with Ginny please?

Clara took in what they were saying. The girl was dead. But if it was a seizure why was there so much blood? What was she a witness to? Where were the children?

Yes, I'll take care of that, of course.

Ginny leaned in close. Listen, you wrap her up in some-thing and I'll come to help you carry her upstairs in a minute. None of the men can do it because they've got to keep order down here. It could turn nasty.

No, of course not. Clara replied. She shouldered the girl and half-walked her into the exhibit room. She lay her down gently on the floor and was startled to feel hot breath on her neck. She knew there were no cameras down there, for obvious reasons. There was a big glass case in the room, and Clara rolled the girl into it. She was so tiny that Clara could do it, even though she was sweating with effort. Clara pulled her own fox mask off and swapped it with the wolf mask the dead girl had been wearing all night. Next she pulled a human skeleton from one of the other cases and bundled it into three sheets. She was done by the time Ginny managed to get away. They were met at the top of the stairs by two guards, who, in one expert motion, took the bundle from them and bore it away.

I'm going. Ginny said. I don't want to be here when things get ugly. You should come too.

I'm going to check on the kids. What if they saw some-thing?

It's not safe.

Exactly.

Okay Clara. It's up to you.

Bye.

Bye. Ginny kissed her on the cheek and walked off down the corridor, buzzing to be let out at the end.

What can I do? thought Clara. I'd better go and see how she is at least. She made her way back down the steps to the basement room, the door clanging shut behind her. When she got to the exhibit room, there was no one there. She was so relieved she could have cried. She walked over to the big glass case and crawled inside, not removing the sheet.

Ava? Jonny? Clara saw them imperfectly in the half light.

Jonny's with the fox, he might die! Ava wailed.

Jonny was curled with his hands around the woman's waist. He was fast asleep.

Shhh Ava, we don't want to wake the fox up.

Ok. Ava whispered.

Listen Ava; can you do something for me? Can you stay in this case, really still and quiet and I promise I'll take the fox away?

Okay. Ava was shaking.

Clara climbed out of the case and walked into the main room. She signalled to Jed.

Jed, listen, Jonny saw something and he got upset. Can you ask the guards to meet me and I'll take the kids home in a taxi?

You can take Jonny home, but you've got to leave Ava here, she's got to come in at the end. It's a delicate situation here.

Okay, then I'll put Jonny in a cab and come back to look after Ava.

It's up to you. I'm busy now.

Ok.

Clara went back to the exhibit room and pulled the woman in the silver dress out by her legs. She pulled Jonny out too. She slapped the woman in the face several times.

Wake up, wake up.

The woman sat up and vomited profusely. Before she'd finished, Clara leaned into her and spoke to her.

They think you're dead, I'm going to help you get out but you have to pretend to be me. Do you understand?

The woman nodded. She bent her head and dry heaved. She started to lie back down. Clara slapped her again.

No. You have to stay awake. Keep this mask on and wear these clothes. I'll stay in the wrap.

The woman seemed to understand.

But how will you get out?

Don't worry about me.

Clara took a towel from her vanity case and helped the

woman to clean herself up before she got dressed. Clara balled up the silver dress covered in blood and vomit and threw them in the corner.

Just hold Jonny in your arms and don't say anything, they'll put you in a cab. Make sure you keep the coat on over your shoulders in case the blood seeps out.

What if he wakes up?

He won't. He's been sedated. When you get to his house just run. Go back to wherever you came from.

Thanks, I will. What's your name?

Clara.

I'm Lou.

Goodbye Lou.

Goodbye Clara.

The woman used all her strength to carry the sleeping child and walked up the stairs. Clara heard the guard address her and the door clang shut again. She was shaking by now and as she clambered back inside the glass case she tried to breathe slowly, to avoid scaring Ava.

Is Jonny okay?

Jonny's fine, he's gone home in a taxi.

Where's the fox?

She went back to her cubs. It's all fine.

Will you hold my hand?

Of course I will.

Clara lay down in the glass case, next to Ava and held her hand while they waited for her big appearance, her star turn.